SEASON OF MARTYRDOM

# SEASON OF MARTYRDOM

## JAMAL NAJI

*Translated by* **Paula Haydar**

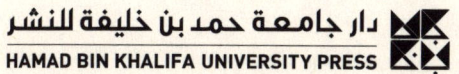

Hamad Bin Khalifa University Press
P O Box 5825
Doha, Qatar

www.hbkupress.com

Copyright © Jamal Naji, 2015
Translation © Paula Haydar, 2016

All rights reserved.

First published in Arabic as *Mawsim Al-Houriyyat* in 2015 by
Hamad Bin Khalifa University Press.

No part of this publication may be reproduced or transmitted
in any form or by any means, electronic or mechanical,
including photocopying, recording, or any information
storage or retrieval system, without prior permission
in writing from the publishers.

No responsibility for loss caused to any individual or organization
acting on or refraining from action as a result of the material in
this publication can be accepted by HBKU Press or the author.

ISBN: 9789927118982

---

**Qatar National Library Cataloging-in-Publication (CIP)**

Naji, Jamal, author.

[موسم الحوريات]. English

  Season of martyrdom / Jamal Naji ; translated by Paula Haydar. - Doha : Hamad Bin Khalifa University Press, 2018.

  pages ; cm

ISBN : 978-992-711-898-2 (pbk.)

1. Short stories, Arabic. 2. Fathers and sons – Fiction. 3. Islamic fundamentalism -- Fiction. 4. Revenge – Fiction. 5. Ethnic conflict – Fiction. I. Haydar, Paula, translator. II. Title.

PJ7852.A5192 S47 2018
892.736 – dc 23

# Sari Abu Amineh

It never crossed my mind that the surprise party I planned for the evening of Fawaz Basha's sixtieth birthday could possibly lead to so many unfathomable twists and turns.

It seems that on that sweltering June night I completely lost my poise and forgot to think things through. It was the first time I'd ever neglected to submit a matter of such high importance to scrutiny before making a decision about it.

It has always been part of my daily routine to dedicate half an hour every morning to singling out the most important events for the day ahead. I always immerse myself in all the related details and implications of each event, and then I decide on a course of action.

But in all my excitement over the surprise I was preparing for the night of Fawaz Basha's birthday, I overlooked that crucial step. It was one of the extremely rare situations when I felt myself being drawn into doing something, involuntarily, as if guided by some unseen force.

Fawaz Basha – of course – had not himself invited the guests who came to his house bearing expensive gifts in order to congratulate him for having reached the sixtieth year of his long, long life.

I was the one who called his friends to remind them of the happy occasion, and as it turned out, they all had remembered. I invited businessmen, journalists, managers and officials; I called them all in my capacity as director of public relations. That was the title the Basha had given me, but that's not exactly what I was. Maybe I was bigger than a public relations director, considering the kinds of important and sensitive matters I was assigned, which made it nearly impossible to describe my job with a title like the ones given to the managers and employees of his companies and offices scattered throughout Jordan and abroad.

Preparations for the party – which was to be held at the Basha's expansive estate situated atop a high hill due west of Amman, overlooking the Kamaliyya area to the east and the villages and steep winding roads of the city of Salt to the west – were being taken care of by one of the catering companies that specialize in weddings, birthdays, and other celebrations.

All of the guests were seated around a long rectangular collection of tables that accommodated thirty-one people – everyone that is except Uroub the fortune-teller. For her I had set a special place in the corner beside the Basha's seat behind the fountain. The fountain sculpture hosted a gathering of crystal *houris* – virginal nymphs – nestled together and pouring water from their transparent palms into the wide round basin. It was set up amidst the grassy green walkways out in the garden, which was enclosed inside a fancy braided wrought iron fence studded with brass stars and with sharp spears for posts.

The party was a joyful acknowledgement of the genetic predisposition to good health that had afforded the Basha the chance to reach age sixty without the least sign of illness or other form of physical frailty that might slow him down. And it was to acknowledge, too, the resilience of his marriage to Mrs Samah Shahadeh, and their good fortune for having stayed together thirty-three years.

The Basha sat at the head of the table beside his elegant wife, conversing with her and smiling in a manner that reflected the perfect state of harmony between them. His wife, with her cascading hairdo and gown that reminded one of the leaves of a banana tree for both its color and its form, was smiling away, her lips painted with a sort of dusky olive shade of lipstick, and returning the compliments she received from the women and men in attendance.

From time to time, however, she would cautiously look over at a friendly Persian cat with wooly white fur that one of the guests had brought with her to the party.

One could not help noticing that the organizers had been intent on displaying all sorts of examples of wealth and luxury. Everything looked valuable and high class: the long table draped in its pearl-white tablecloth with embroidered edges, the plates resting on wine-colored silk placemats, the shiny gilded bowls, the crystal vases holding tulips the color of the sun, the emerald-tinted long-stemmed glasses with their antique etchings. And near the table were statues of eagles swooping down on circular stone bases and marble pillars wrapped in awe-inspiring sashes. And then there were the two Philippine maids and the five local women hired to serve the guests as well, in their mini-skirts and revealing blouses.

It was a very promising beginning to a birthday party that was sure to be a success. The Basha and his wife were exchanging pleasantries with their guests, complimenting them with refinement and joining in on their conversations.

But then something happened that brought all my high expectations crashing down, and turned my happy surprise into an evil curse – on me and on the Basha, too.

When it was time for Uroub the fortune-teller to appear, she came toward us with a level of confidence rarely possessed by a woman.

She wore a black hair tie about an inch thick over her forehead and head. Her wiry and uncombed jet-black hair dangled out from under it, as did the interlocking silver earrings hanging from her earlobes. Below that was a blue scarf coiled around her neck, draped over a shiny black dress with flowing belle sleeves. The dress looked more like an evening gown than something a fortune-teller would wear while reading palms and predicting people's futures. She certainly drew the attention of the women and men seated around the table when she greeted them with a measured smile and a careful nod of her head. They all began whispering and murmuring the moment she shook Mrs Samah's hand and then greeted the Basha with a respectful curtsy before taking her seat beside him.

It seemed the guests were able to mask their curiosity quickly by occupying themselves with the drinks and hors d'oeuvres that preceded the cutting of the birthday cake. They struck up conversations about the unfolding Arab Spring and the terrible violence in Syria and speculated about the potential spillover effect on Jordan, their teeth chomping all the while on those little bites of food that ruin a person's appetite.

Most likely they did not notice the direction the conversation was taking at the head of the table behind the fountain of *houris*, between the Basha and the fortune-teller who was scrutinizing his face with her pitch-black eyes outlined with a light shadow of kohl. She leaned in very close to him and softly said – I could barely hear her even though I was standing in the empty space right behind them – "Today is not your birthday, sir."

He raised his thick eyebrows, glanced at his wife, looked at Uroub and said, with a chuckle, "If today is not my birthday, then what is it, the Day of Resurrection?"

Mrs Samah was following what was transpiring with much concern, and her concern only grew when Uroub smiled and said, "Cancer is not your astrological sign, sir. This birthdate of yours which falls on the twenty-fourth of June has nothing to do with you. You are a Leo. Your birth records are in error."

She removed the blue scarf from her neck and laid it flat on her knees. She regarded him again with those pitch-black eyes.

"The awe that surrounds you," she said, "is not a characteristic of Cancer or of any other sign for that matter. If you were to let your hair grow, it would grow all around your face and you would look just like a lion. Your ruddy complexion is controlled by the sun, a symbol of power and influence, not by the moon that lives by the sun's light. The sun is your star and your planet.

"Moreover, there are three qualities found in Cancers that you do not possess: Cancers are dreamers, while you are analytical; Cancers adore children, but you cannot stand them; and Cancers are stingy, whereas you are very generous and giving."

He nodded his head as if to show he agreed with what she was saying. He and his wife exchanged glances. He cleared his throat and then his voice came out from under his mustache effortlessly, "OK. And what about my fortune? What's in store for me in the coming days and years?"

She put her hands on each side of her head. "Sir, the only way to tell your future is by looking at your palms, but you Leos only hear what you want to hear."

He looked at me as if to ask about this revelation that had changed the rhythm of his evening. When I leaned in closer he whispered in my ear, "I'll be waiting for you in my office."

Then he got up and headed down one of the corridors leading to his office and I followed. When I stood before him he clasped his hands behind his back and began pacing as he usually did whenever he was nervous about something.

I noticed that the legs of his trousers were so long they covered his shoes entirely, and when he turned around and faced me I could see that his belt was tightened below his belly that I now noticed had developed a bit of a paunch.

"This is quite a surprise," he said to me in an inquiring tone. "Where did you get this fortune-teller from?"

"I thought this kind of thing appealed to you, so I arranged for her to come without asking permission first. I wanted it to be a nice surprise on your birthday. She's from Morocco, and if you don't like what she is saying, I can have the driver take her back to her hotel immediately. We'll forget she ever set foot in your hospitable home. But I should tell you that it was very difficult getting her here for the party. I stumbled upon her by chance. She told me she would only be in Amman for two days and on the first day she met with a very important personality whose identity I have been unable to determine. I found out that the same night she traveled south of the Dead Sea accompanied by three of that same person's bodyguards and stayed the whole night studying the stars until dawn. Tomorrow she is headed to Caracas to visit a very important man there suffering from an incurable disease, and after that she will fly out to Brunei. That is what she said."

"She's that important?" he asked, raising his eyebrows with a show of interest.

"Yes. And there is more. She possesses uncanny abilities. I found out she predicted that Nicolas Sarkozy would win the French elections seventy days prior to his being nominated as a candidate. It was all over the French papers at the time. She also foretold Qaddafi's fall from power a month before the Libyan revolution. And she told me that the people of Syria would be embroiled in conflict tenfold, meaning ten years, and would be divided fourfold and will rebuild what the war has destroyed tenfold. And the people of Iraq would witness a fire unlike any the human race has ever seen before."

"True I'm interested in this type of thing, but . . . 'Soothsayers speak lies, even if their predictions come true . . .' Remember?"

"That only confirms that what they say does come true sometimes, sir."

He was silent. Then he asked, "Do you want her to read my fortune and speak about my future in front of all my guests?"

"This is what I was going to warn you about, but I didn't dare. If you wish, I can request for her to come here to your office so you can sit with her in private and hear her predictions."

He assented with a nod of his head, without saying a word. Before I started heading back to the banquet table behind the fountain of *houris*, he said to me, "By the way, what she said about my birthday and astrological sign might actually be true."

I went back to the party to find Uroub engaged in quiet conversation with Mrs Samah; the other guests were carrying on about politics and business. Politicians, businessmen, and rich people – clearly the party had given them the perfect opportunity to do some networking and maybe even shake on a few deals.

Shock was all over Mrs Samah's face; her expression had changed completely, as if her real face had been snatched away, and her eyes were nailed open in disbelief.

Mrs Samah loved surprises and distractions; she also loved swimming, classical music, and travel. She hated house pets and was one of the most patient and understanding people I've ever seen, but she couldn't stand talk of politics or get involved in its dark back-alleys. She told me one time that she was much too refined to have anything to do with politics.

She said that, in fact, in the presence of one of the Basha's acquaintances who was a government minister, who smiled and responded, "You are absolutely right, Mrs Samah."

I wasn't able to make out what Uroub was saying. I waited a little for Uroub to stop talking and then I whispered in her ear. She excused herself from Mrs Samah and joined me.

As I walked beside Uroub I noticed that her clothing made a swishing sound and released a pleasant fragrance. But most likely it wasn't perfume; it smelled more like essential oil.

The Basha greeted her respectfully and seated her in the chair across from his. Then he asked me to stay with them.

He looked her over carefully – her eyes, her body – with his big, wide eyes. The Basha's large brown eyes had the ability to swivel inside their sockets with great ease, and they had an amazing capacity to remain fixed and peer into things and people and faces in a disconcerting manner.

Despite that, Uroub did not display the least bit of uneasiness when her eyes met his. With an air of delight, she said, "Open your palms, sir."

He looked at me and smiled, and I smiled back encouragingly. He opened his palms and she took them into her hands and began touching them and examining them: the lines of the palms, the hills and valleys, the fingertips, the knuckles, the grooves of the fingernails. She examined every part of his palms with her tapered fingers. While staring at her fingers I noticed that the gold ring on her ring finger was in the shape of a scarab. I also noted while looking at the side of her head that her dark face had sharp features and her looks were nothing like the looks of women I had come to know over the course of my life. There was something different about her.

As for her age, I guessed she was forty-five at most.

## Samah Shahadeh

Uroub. Uroub.

That fortune-teller drove me insane with what she said about the dream I had the night before my husband Fawaz's birthday party.

She said some obscure and frightening things. It is quite possible of course, though I doubt it, that she got information about me and my husband ahead of time. Information nowadays is readily available with the help of the Internet. All astrologers or fortune-tellers need is people's names and they can easily find out their history and relationships, can find pictures of them in groups or individually – all before sitting down with them to discuss their past and future. We are living in the third millennium, a time in which fortune-tellers are in high demand, to the point where some leaders and heads of state seek their advice before making important decisions.

In spite of all this, some fortune-tellers elicit my curiosity and my anxiety, too, especially when something close to what they predict comes true. Or something related to their predictions, no matter how slight.

Uroub was nothing like the other fortune-tellers I had encountered.

Each fortune-teller has her own spiritual imprint. At least this was the impression I got whenever I met one.

First of all, Uroub was a beautiful woman, with an enviable liveliness. Usually fortune-tellers and palm readers are old and wrinkled with disheveled hair.

In my eye, Uroub was as bright and shiny as the little pearl bead attached to her left nostril, and her hair was pitch-black and curled in a style that flattered her face beautifully.

Uroub's body was tight and toned; she didn't look more than forty years old at most. It reminded me of my own ripening body back when I was forty years old.

The day after the party I told Fawaz that Uroub ought to be a dancer with that slender figure of hers, and her well-proportioned body, and her bewitching smile. Maybe she had been a dancer before becoming a fortune-teller.

He asked me if what I was saying was a compliment or an insult.

And second of all, Uroub had the ability to soothe one's spirit and calm one's nerves with that deep voice of hers that crept its way into my soul, silenced my tongue, and shattered my concentration.

I felt as though my soul had quieted down, gone limp, and was being held captive in her cage – despite all the noise of the guests – as if enveloped and cradled by her words and the tone of her voice.

Her voice emanated from a very deep place within her soul.

I got the feeling her inner self was a vast expanse full of never-ending distances.

Her fingers tickled the tips and edges of my fingers and fondled the palm of my hand, sending chills up and down my entire being. Things seemed like a puff of flimsy fluffed up wool; I felt weightless.

It was delightful.

It had been a very long time since I'd felt those sensations whose sweet wellsprings I thought, in my advanced age, had long since dried up.

I got Uroub's personal phone number.

And third of all, she figured out that my husband is a Leo, not a Cancer as he had presumed.

I had told him once that I thought he was more like a Leo than a Cancer, but he didn't react.

His date of birth was not really certain, because his father did not register it at the time of his birth via a neighborhood midwife. It was registered later on using a rough estimate.

That is what his late mother told me before she died of lung cancer nine years after we got married – may God rest her soul.

## Sari Abu Amineh

Uroub sighed and then began an incantation seeking God's protection from the devil, in a deep, undulating tone that transformed the Basha into a silent listener who didn't make a peep or move in the slightest, except to wrinkle his thick eyebrows together at that very moment. His eyes, however, remained fixed on Uroub's face.

She said to him, "Sir, people love to hear good news and hate to hear anything unpleasant. This is what causes them to lose sight of the truth, in favor of a moment's satisfaction and happiness."

He smiled at her and said, "Tell me what you see, no matter what it is, and you will have whatever you want, no matter how much it is."

She nodded her head calmly.

"Your wealth will increase in heaps and piles, and God will open for you the doors of an obscure and enticing business venture that will bring you riches beyond compare, and those people who seek you out and who envy you will also grow in number."

"That's what all the fortune-tellers and astrologers say," he said in a haughty tone.

She sighed and continued on as if she hadn't heard him. "But you will experience a difficult year. The heavens that have been otherwise preoccupied and have left you alone all the days of your life, are going to pounce on you in your coming days and do as they please, interfering in your life in order to uphold the fate that awaits you."

Then she cupped her palm behind her left ear and said, tenderly, "I can almost hear the sound of fate's hoofs galloping across the plains of your coming days. You must take heed against this year, sir. It is the year of your sorrow."

Then the expression on her face made her look like she was seeing the events of his future unfold before her very eyes.

"There is only one person in this world who is of your own flesh and blood: your son, who is lost out there somewhere in God's forsaken universe. But he will appear to you, pained by the silent fire that has been burning within him for a very long time, a fire buried deep inside him. I can nearly hear his cries reverberating in the heavens with my own ears. He will appear to you because your death will come at his hands."

The Basha let out a listless laugh. "I have no children. My wife cannot conceive. But I wish I did have a son, even if my death were to come at his hands!"

She continued, showing no sign of his words having had the slightest effect on her. "Sir, you must seek out and find this son before he comes for you."

What surprised me was the way the smile vanished from the Basha's face, leaving behind the look of someone who believed the prediction would come true.

"And what else do you see in my future?"

"This son of yours is very bold. Nothing can hold him back and blood will not deter him from getting what he wants. He is living in a different era than yours, sir."

The Basha and Uroub exchanged glances I couldn't interpret. I felt there was some sort of unspoken dialogue transpiring between them.

"And where is this son?" he asked.

She raised her palms to the heavens in a prayer-like gesture and then answered, "Heaven has closed its doors, but I thank God, the

Hidden One, the Noble One, for opening my heart and allowing me to see what I have seen of your future."

Then she repeated what she had said but with more emphasis this time. "Do not forget, sir. You must find this son before he finds you."

He looked at me, then at her. He rose from his seat and paced back and forth with his hands clasped behind his back as he spoke to her. "OK. Let's suppose that what you say is true and that what you predict will happen happens. Is there any way to change this fate?"

She answered, after letting out a sigh, "I am but one of God's weak servants, sir. I have no power to alter the fates or to approach their impenetrable fortresses."

She was silent for a moment and then added, "Our great sage and source of all authority in India, Harsha al-Hakim, is the only one who can answer your question for you. He is the only one who is able to speak directly to the fates and can attempt to traverse their fortresses by his works. Who knows? Perhaps they will turn their great locks and open their gates to you."

The Basha stood there in all his greatness, not moving. He looked pale and worried. As for me, I felt I'd made the biggest mistake of my life bringing Uroub to this occasion. I feigned a smile and said, "Mr Basha, sir, this whole matter is nothing more than an unlikely surprise I prepared for you on your birthday. Don't forget that men such as yourself determine the course of fate. You're outside the realm of fortunes and fortune-telling."

But the sudden look he gave me silenced me at once. I knew when I should be quiet in the presence of that man who now seemed very different from the man I had known before.

## Samah Shahadeh

Ever since I was a small child and even as I have reached the age of fifty-seven, I have always enjoyed listening to astrologers and fortune-tellers.

I cannot resist the possibility of knowing the future, even if it comes through fortune-tellers.

But I'm afraid of the way they look into my eyes when they talk, as if creeping right inside my brain. And I'm also afraid of the timbre of their voices, which inspires a mysterious feeling of awe.

My mother knew astrologers and fortune-tellers in Beirut, Cairo, Marrakesh, Athens, Budapest, and other cities. More than once during my childhood she brought me with her on trips to those cities, and every time she insisted on having her fortune read – and mine, too.

None of those fortune-tellers were right except for one we met in Budapest a quarter century ago who had only one eye. He told her that one of her spinster sisters was going to get married within a year, and it actually happened. My aunt got married about seven months after we got back, at the age of forty-three.

My father – may God give him a long life – never believed in astrologers or fortune-tellers or soothsayers. He used to call them "soul foxes" and would comment on my mother's tendency to be swept away by them, telling her, "Fine. Go ahead and listen to them if it's going to improve your mood."

In my case, none of the fortune-tellers' predictions ever came completely true, only partially true. But I would cling to those bits and pieces nevertheless because there were things I was able to know before they happened, no matter how insignificant they were.

I asked Uroub to interpret a worrisome dream I had the night before she came to our house. In the dream I saw a wall in our garden. It broke open and a cat jumped out from inside.

"And she shakes her head, right?" Uroub said, completing the dream for me.

"Yes," I said, surprised.

"What color was it?" she asked.

"Gray," I answered.

"You are going to find out about a secret that has been kept from you for many years and it will have a major effect on your life in the future."

Totally bewildered, I asked, "How did you know what I saw in my dream?"

"How I knew is not important, madame. The important thing is the cat came back to life."

"What is this secret that I will discover?" I asked her. "I have no secrets and my husband is completely open to me, like the palm of my hand."

"Every creature has its hidden things. Even the moon has a side we don't see."

When she read my palm, she told me it was one in a long chain of palms on which riches poured down in torrents for decades, and the rain was still soaking me and soaking my husband along with me.

I remembered that Fawaz had nothing when he married me. Thanks to my father and his care and attention, Fawaz became a wealthy and influential man, and a Basha.

"And what about the gray cat?" I asked.

"Most likely it was not gray."

"I remember it well. It was gray," I said.

"All cats look gray at night, madame."

I noticed afterwards that all cats do look gray at night, no matter what color they are.

# Sari Abu Amineh

I must bear the fallout of the surprise I prepared for the Basha, who became a completely different person overnight. The image of him in my mind turned into a double-image after that. I would recall how he was after his meeting with Uroub, but then, with pain, remember his other image whenever I discussed with him some topic or project that had preceded his meeting with Uroub.

The Basha believed in the tangible things in life. That's how I've known him to be since starting to work for him. He had an analytical mind. (Uroub said that, too!) But sometimes he would ask me to read his horoscope in the newspapers. A few times I accompanied him on trips to Europe and Asia and occasionally he would seek out fortune-tellers to have them do readings for him. He told me he picked up an interest in them from his wife, Mrs Samah, the daughter of the Grand Basha Nayef Shahadeh, whose daily cigar, I discovered, cost 100 dinars.

There was an obscure space between Samah's father and Fawaz Basha. A space I was never able to decipher, despite all the faith and good graces bestowed on me by both men.

But the Basha's interest in fortune-tellers had begun only ten years earlier, during a visit to the Acropolis Museum in Athens where he met a fortune-teller with flowing hair and sagging breasts who spoke to him in her weary voice. "Luck will be in your favor in a competition between you and a high-ranking man, because he will be the one to take the seat, not you."

"How can luck be in my favor if he is the one who takes the seat and not me?" he asked her.

"It's a different seat than the one you have in mind," she answered.

Some of what she said ended up coming true. A currency trader and importer of Swiss gold who was competing with one of the Basha's companies got in a car crash with a truck while driving between Zurich and Basel on a business trip. He was sent back to Amman and he's been in a wheelchair ever since.

When the Basha heard what happened to that man he said to me in amazement, "That is the seat the Acropolis fortune-teller predicted!"

After that he had his fortune read a lot, but none of the predictions came true, so his interest in them waned.

But after meeting Uroub, he changed. If I hadn't seen it with my own eyes and hadn't been personally involved in it, I would never have believed that Basha Fawaz, after all the lies and nonsense he'd heard before, would believe a fortune-teller who'd breezed into town to tell him that his birthday and astrological sign were wrong, that he had a son, and that that son was going to bring about his demise.

The following week, after finishing one of those closed-door meetings of his – the kind he only allows people who are directly involved in to attend while their drivers and attendants wait for them outside – he called me and asked me to come to his office right away.

I felt that the Basha's life was brimming with secrets. Maybe I needed to peruse all the pages of his past and his present; I needed to gather up all the keys that could open the locked rooms of his life.

But that was precisely what could not happen.

For he was – as far as I knew – much too smart to allow all the keys giving access to his world to be gathered in one place.

Fifteen minutes after his call, I arrived at his office. He sat me down beside him.

He told me to find a woman by the name of Muntaha al-Rayyeh. He recalled that she used to live in the Swayleh area north of Amman. She had worked for one of his companies thirty years earlier, and he'd slept with her at the time.

"Give me a few days," I said. "I'll have a full report on her for you."

He looked directly into my eyes and said, "You do not seem surprised. Did you know about my relationship with this woman?"

"Of course not, Basha, sir, but these things happen with men all the time."

He finally broke his stare. Then he instructed me to establish whether that woman, Muntaha al-Rayyeh, had gotten pregnant from him or not, and if I happened to run into her and it appeared he did indeed have an illegitimate child from her, then I should find out where this son was, what his name was, and try to meet him, get a picture of him, and probe him, probe his thoughts, find out if he knew who his real father was.

But before all that, I was to make preparations for a trip I would be accompanying him on to India to meet the sage Harsha al-Hakim, who dwelled in the Maharashtra mountains, near the Arabian Sea.

# Samah Shahadeh

I asked Fawaz what Uroub had said to him. He grinned so wide I could see all his white teeth and his pink gums below his mustache, too. "You know fortune-tellers are full of lies."

I had seen that grin once before, about thirty years earlier, and at the time it stirred up in me many unanswered questions. He had come back from Paris missing me tremendously; he tore off my clothes the moment he arrived. He made love to me with the vigor and fire of a young man, after having been away from me for ten days. When he was finished, he got up and walked to the bathroom and I could see two long scratches down his back. When I asked him about them, he smiled, and I could see his teeth and his gums, which were much healthier and pinker back then. He told me that the Turkish masseur from the hotel fitness center was extremely thorough and scrubbed him with loofah and pumice.

That same grin that had been etched in my memory thirty years ago reappeared when I asked him what Uroub had said to him.

He had spent quite some time alone with her and Sari in his office before coming back to join his guests at the party.

It was possible she said something to him worth being concerned about.

"And what lies did she tell you, exactly?" I asked.

"She said I was going to die at the hands of a thirty-year-old man."

I was startled. "We should look to God to know our future, not to her. How dare she?"

He smiled. "I told you it was a bunch of lies."

I grumbled. "But I think she got to the truth about your astrological sign. Haven't I told you before that you're more like a Leo than a Cancer?"

He answered with a single word: "Maybe."

I asked Sari what Uroub had said to Fawaz and he told me he hadn't been able to hear her, because he was too busy taking care of party matters and the needs of the guests that night.

Sari was the one person who was never too busy for things having to do with the Basha.

# Sari Abu Amineh

On our way from Amman to Mumbai, at an altitude of 30,000 feet above sea level and after gulping down two glasses of wine, the Basha said, "I told you before, what Uroub said about my having an illegitimate son might be true. Isn't that enough to make me think the part about my demise might also be true?"

Trying to appease him, I said, "But Basha, she might not have gotten pregnant from you."

He responded very quickly, "A man who can't control himself in bed knows the consequences of going all the way with a woman; and it's even worse for a man who tends to come quickly. I'm sure you know what I'm talking about."

"Even in this case," I said, "not every act of intercourse leads to conception. You only slept with her one time as far as I understand it."

He sighed. "It was a few times. And my intuition tells me it's not as you're suggesting. And I always trust my intuition." Then he peered into my face and gave a wide wine-stained smile. "Do you believe in fate?"

"Not really," I answered. "But I live in constant fear of it."

I felt the depth of the anxiety that was oppressing him, as though what I'd done in bringing Uroub was analogous to someone wanting to apply kohl to the eyelids and gouging out the eyeballs in the process.

I said, "It could just be a prediction that happened to coincide with a truth you were hiding all along."

"And what she said about my sign could also be true," he said with conviction, "most likely is true."

He was speaking like someone who had finally caught on to something he'd failed to grasp for years, so he grabbed it tightly and showed no sign of relinquishing it.

We arrived at Mumbai airport in the morning. It was hot, humid, and sticky, and I got the feeling that sounds had a different rhythm to them there than in the other cities I'd traveled to. It was the sound of commotion with an underlying and nearly constant high-speed din.

An hour after we arrived, we took off in an Air India plane to the city of Aurangabad. It was an old and noisy plane with no distinction between first class and tourist class except that they supplied us with newspapers and magazines.

In Aurangabad we stayed in a hotel with lush green courtyards called the Lemon Tree Hotel. We dropped our luggage in our rooms and then set out for the Ajanta Temples, which took us fifty minutes to reach in the Jeep we picked up at the hotel car rental office.

The road trip gave me the fright of my life. My heart pounded in my chest like a trapped bird. The driver of the Jeep was obsessed with speed, and with the incessant Hindi songs that stopped only after the Basha spoke sternly to him in English. And that was not all. He was also quite adventurous with his driving, swerving around corners and hairpin turns on those mountainous roads on the precipice of deep valleys. Despite all our attempts to convince him we were not in a hurry and that in any case he would be waiting for us while we went on our visit so he could take us back to the hotel, that olive-skinned driver with the shiny black hair parted down the middle didn't take heed.

We reached the stone-carved Ajanta Temples, and I felt the presence of a terrifying silence in that place, despite the numerous Indian and foreign visitors who had come to see the rows of striped temples chiseled into the foot of the mountain. Something compelled me to silent contemplation. Even the Basha looked humbled and weak in that awesome place.

But the Ajanta Temples were not our final destination. We were headed to the abode of the sage Harsha al-Hakim, which was located on a hilltop three valleys and two rocky hills south of the temples.

The driver handed us over to a tall lanky tour guide who worked in the area, and then he disappeared inside the temples to wait until we came back.

We were surprised to discover that reaching the sage's headquarters required a forty-minute walk, and we had thought the road would be paved or at least level, but all we found were narrow paths winding through the mountains and valleys.

Before we set out, the guide advised us to buy a couple of straw hats for protection from the sun and two bottles of cold water.

We walked behind him down rocky paths and other sandy paths that were surrounded by tall pine and almond trees. Groups of monkeys holding their young crouched on the hills and nearby rocks, eyeing us curiously.

Trying to lighten things up on our difficult trek, I said, "I feel like I really needed this trip, in order to see things I haven't been used to seeing."

The Basha answered, panting, "I don't think I will forget this trip as long as I live."

He was walking ahead of me in his white shirt and khaki pants. From behind, his head looked square to me, and his shoulders broad, and his rear end seemed to be protruding backwards.

The sky was an expanse of clear blue, broken by mountains adorned with green trees. Our clothes were soaked with sweat, to the point that I thought maybe the slight paunch that had developed at my waistline had melted away during our walk. As for the Basha, he stopped every so often to drink a little bit of water, swish it around in his mouth, and sprinkle some over his head before starting up again.

At the foot of a stone hill, the entrance to Harsha al-Hakim's abode appeared before us, carved into the stone and with engravings on both sides. Along the top of the entranceway were little statues stuck together and carved into the stone. The sound of distant melodies reached us, as if they'd been sent from above.

When we neared the entrance we were surprised to find an old man dressed in white and sitting on a boulder a few meters away. Before him was a smoldering fire over which he was turning a two-meter-long snake that writhed in the flames but didn't die. We stopped to get a good look at this strange scene. Still panting, the Basha asked the young guide, "What is that old man doing to the snake?"

"Bathing him," he answered. "It's a fire snake."

"Don't his hands get burned?" I asked. "Doesn't the snake get burned?"

"It is a heatless fire."

I smelled a new scent in that place, something close to the odor released when bark is peeled from a tree. While I was looking around trying to locate the source of the scent, a bearded man in his fifties suddenly came out from inside the abode, leaning on a primitive staff. His features and sunburned skin inspired a sense of humility.

He asked us in English for our names, the purpose of our visit, and who had referred us, so I explained to him why we had come and I mentioned the name of Uroub, the Moroccan woman. He nodded his head and told us to follow him.

The top of the entrance door was very low, not more than a meter and a half high, so we were forced to duck down behind him as he led us to an area where there were rows of benches chiseled into the stone. He asked us to wait there and headed down a narrow corridor.

We sat on the benches. I looked into the Basha's face, expecting to see him worried and distressed in this strange world we found ourselves in, but he appeared to be at ease and content. He spoke to me in a hushed voice.

"No matter what the outcome of this trip, I feel like I'm living another life, a calm life far away from all the noise and hypocrisy of everyone in the city. Have you ever experienced such cosmic tranquility before?"

I responded in a hushed voice, too. "I feel a certain humility here. This place inspires awe and reverence."

The attendant came back and ushered us down the narrow corridor to where Harsha al-Hakim was.

It was clear that the old man sitting behind the speckled stone table was Al-Hakim and the bearded man sitting beside him was the interpreter who would translate from Hindi into English.

There were no windows inside the cave, and no other sources of light, and so I was amazed there was so much daylight streaming in. I noticed that the Basha looked on in total awe at this new miracle.

Harsha al-Hakim's face and his general appearance reminded me of the image that had formed in my imagination as a child of those legendary, ancient peoples who lived well into their hundreds.

I felt as though the man had surpassed all the statistics to do with longevity and life expectancy. He wore a white Indian cap and there was an ethereal glow that emanated from his wrinkled face. His beard was white and thick and ran together with his mustache and sideburns. It actually covered so much of his face that only a small triangular patch encompassing his eyes, the area around his nose, and the line of his quivering lips, was left bare.

He was seated on the floor with his legs crossed, behind a table which provided a resting place for his sharp elbows and stick-like arms. He held a set of prayer beads between his skinny fingers that dangled over the edge of the table.

He signaled with his eyes for us to sit down cross-legged before him. He looked into the Basha's face, but did not look into mine. He seemed able to ascertain our relative importance from the way we entered and sat down.

The Basha cleared his throat and recounted his story for Harsha al-Hakim and told him all about what Uroub the fortune-teller said the night of his sixtieth birthday party. As soon as he finished, the translator began performing his task.

There was total silence. Al-Hakim shut his eyes, lowered his head and started playing with the beads. Meanwhile, the Basha turned his head and stared at the stone walls that were dispersing light throughout the place, as if to give Al-Hakim a chance to think before announcing his verdict.

Al-Hakim said solemnly, "Uroub has permission to speak on our behalf. What she has told you is with our permission. It is your fate, and there is no way to escape from it. Why did you come?"

"She said you have a way to change fate," the Basha answered. "I don't care how much money it will cost me. I want to change my fate if you confirm what Uroub predicted. Is it in your power to change fate?"

## Muntaha al-Rayyeh

I knew Fawaz al-Shardah (now they call him the Basha) from the Malco Stock Company in the Shmeisani area of Amman, behind the white-collar union complex.

How I wish I had never met him.

That was thirty years ago.

He was the biggest shareholder in the company and he used to visit once every two or three months.

I worked as a typist for the company, at a very low salary, because I never continued my studies after graduating from junior college.

One day, with a frown, my boss dropped off a large batch of paperwork he wanted me to process before leaving for the day.

We used to call that boss the "Porcupine" because he pricked whoever came close to him. Plus he was short and thin and his hair – black in those days – stood straight up on his head.

I placed the papers in front of me on the desk, grumbling.

Everyone else who worked there left at the end of their shifts while I stayed behind at my desk, all alone except for the company clerk.

An hour later, Fawaz al-Shardah arrived at the office, despite it being past normal business hours.

The clerk greeted him with such exuberance; he might as well have carried him on his back, too. Fawaz ordered him to make two cups of tea – one for him and one for me.

God knows it was pure coincidence, but it completely changed my life.

Did I say coincidence?

I guessed he was around my age, thirty-ish. He had a full head of thick black hair and a broad, white face. He was wearing a coarse brown suit, a white shirt, and a walnut-colored necktie.

I was wearing a dust-colored dress that covered my knees. In those days I got hit on by lots of colleagues and other men at work, asking me out to restaurants, but I never took them up on it. I was afraid of them. They had hungry eyes that would eat me alive if they could. What was worse, any one of them would mean an instant scandal; if I went out with one, the news would spread around the whole company like wildfire. It happened to my friend who worked at the same company and there was a big scandal.

The Porcupine was always commiserating with me about having to fight the traffic between where I lived in Swayleh and the office in Shmeisani, frequently offering to give me rides. He told me he lived on the far end of Swayleh and my house was right on his way to and from the office, but I didn't take his offer. I knew the Porcupine and his intentions very well.

Fawaz approached me. I could smell his strong cologne.

He very casually asked me my name, where I lived, when the firm had hired me. I was sitting at my desk behind an Olivetti typewriter. He kept circling around the desk and around me as he spoke. I felt as though he were tying me up with invisible strings, trapping me in my place.

Despite the fact that he was the same age as me, he seemed much older. He possessed that awe-inspiring air of bosses and rich people, an aura that had nothing to do with age.

He didn't stay circling around me for long.

The clerk came back carrying a tray with two cups of tea with mint. Fawaz gave him some money and said, "You go ahead and drink it. I have an appointment."

On his way out he patted me on the shoulder, praising me for my hard work and willingness to work late, and I thanked him for his kindness. To be precise, his fingers brushed against the skin of my shoulder, just below my neck, but I disregarded that and convinced myself it was merely praise for a hard-working employee.

After he left, I touched my hand against the spot on my shoulder he had brushed with his fingers. My mind felt empty, bare of all thoughts. I scratched my forehead with my red-polished fingernails, and the scent of his cologne came back to me. I sniffed my fingers and the scent was stronger.

My mood changed. I stared straight ahead, without focusing on anything in particular. Even after he'd left, he was still standing there beside me. My neck and my whole body went limp. I wiped my face and brushed off my shoulders, freeing myself of the strings he had wrapped around me.

Then I decided to postpone finishing the paperwork until the next day, forgetting the problems it would cause from the Porcupine, who had hit on me twice before when I first started working there. Once was in his office, as I was bending over to correct a typing error and he put his hand on my knee and clamped hold of it like a pair of pliers, to which I responded by jumping back in alarm. He started laughing childishly, as if he was playing a game. The second time was also in his office. I had arrived early to work because of an easing in the traffic that always determined my daily arrival time. I got there twenty minutes before any other employees, and was surprised to find the Porcupine all alone in his office. I greeted him good morning and he told me I had come just at the right time, handed me a big file, and asked me to find a certain document. I put my purse down and opened up the file. He got up from his chair and left his office. Then he came back and stood right beside me, acting like he was trying to help me search the file. He kept putting his hand on mine, and his bony pelvis bumped against my thigh, so I withdrew my hand and started to leave, but he grabbed me and pushed me up against the wall. Suddenly his rat's mouth was between my breasts. He latched onto me like a tick. I gathered myself and broke free of him all at once. Then I slapped him on the neck. I noticed his face was beet red and he looked startled and rattled.

But he regained his composure and started laughing childishly again, as if he was playing a game.

He must have been around thirty-five years old.

I didn't know who I should complain to about the Porcupine. He was "connected," as I had been told, with a direct relation to Fawaz and many of the higher-ups, one of whom was Nayef Shahadeh, Fawaz's father-in-law.

I applied for many other jobs after that, but didn't hear back from any of them. And so I remained under the Porcupine's command.

After Fawaz left, I grabbed my purse and went home.

My father noticed that something was wrong and asked me what was the matter. All I could think to tell him was that I was tired from work.

My relationship with my father was calm on the outside and complicated on the inside. It was pretty much a one-sided love. He loved me and tried to placate me, but I felt stifled by the fatherly love which came with large doses of over-protectiveness and unsolicited advice.

My mother was very strong and in full control at home. Her constant meddling in my father's personal affairs annoyed him, and he often found reasons to go out or visit relatives, in order to avoid problems with her. But the thing that irritated me was how she always knew what I was thinking, even if I didn't say a word to her.

The day after Fawaz's visit, the Porcupine didn't lecture me like he usually did. Instead, he praised my loyalty and conveyed the praise that had come from Fawaz who – according to the Porcupine – "just happened to be driving by in his car, having turned from the next street over, and decided to drop in for a visit seeing as he thought we were all still working. But then he found you working all by yourself, a mere coincidence."

Then he added, "You're very lucky. He singled you out, finding you there without any of the other girls around. Expect some kind of reward from him. Maybe he will even ask you to lunch one of these days. It's his way of honoring those who do selfless work."

## Sari Abu Amineh

Changing fate. That was the last thing I imagined I would be thinking about while navigating my way through this construction zone called life. However, changing fate was precisely what the Basha wanted, and what we went all the way to India to seek.

"The problem with your situation," Harsha al-Hakim continued, "is that you have come to me from a land teeming with heaven's activities. God began all his activities right there in your homeland; that is what your books say. He created Abraham in Mesopotamia and sent him to Egypt then on to Palestine. Then he created Moses in Egypt and sent him to Palestine. Then he created Jesus the Nazarene in Bethlehem and willed his death in Jerusalem. Then he created Muhammad in Mecca and sent him to Jerusalem, according to your book, and willed his death in the place where he was born.

"Son, in places where heaven's activities are abundant, it is more difficult to interfere with the fates, impossible even, and you have come to me from a land the heavens never tire of roaming through and over which the fates are constantly flapping their wings."

Then he fell silent. A semblance of hopelessness appeared on the Basha's face. As for myself, my feeling of humility grew before Harsha al-Hakim's vast world of knowledge, and before the idea of heavenly activity in our land, which had never occurred to me that way before.

Al-Hakim took in a deep breath through his nose, which looked like a small fig, and resumed speaking to the Basha. "And also, the lives of the rich and powerful do not just belong to them, because the destinies of hundreds or maybe millions of others are tied to them. I know that you have companies and business interests that employ many people, and businesses that provide a living for many families. You are of great importance in your country.

"Your life and death hold sway over those connected to you. If the lives of people such as yourself deviate from fate's course, the entire chain could be broken. The system could be shattered and our existence could go completely out of control. Fate can overlook a common person, because his life doesn't affect the destiny of others. That is what allows common people freedoms that elicit the envy of the rich and powerful. Any one of them can die whenever he likes, and do whatever he wants whenever he wants, because he is just one little cog in the millions and billions of wheels by which the machine of fate rolls along its path. If one breaks or gets off track, it has no effect whatsoever. As for the likes of you, you do not enjoy the luxury of doing what you please. This is a luxury exclusive to commoners. It cannot be loaned out to the rich and powerful."

Then he was silent, and I found myself clearing my throat and saying, "Sir, I know nothing of fate and destiny; next to your vast store of knowledge I am but a simple man living on the outskirts of your wisdom's domain. However, it is true that our Prophet Muhammad, peace be upon him, said, 'Prayer meets the calamity that has been decreed and wrestles with it over that which is between heaven and earth. A battle takes place between them, and if the prayer is stronger, then the calamity is lifted, but if the prayer is weaker, the calamity is brought down, though to a lesser degree.'"

Al-Hakim looked me in the face for the first time since I'd entered his abode. Then he said, "Son, if this encounter takes place, it is governed by fate. And it only concerns the common people. As for the rich and powerful, they are merely creatures living at fate's disposal, creatures whose prayers do nothing to change their destinies. There is a force that reigns over things, an obscure, cosmic force that is not embodied in any one being. And it is not bound by time. Indeed it is outside the boundaries of time as you know it."

Encouraged by this I said, "Please permit me, wise sir, to ask you about your religion?"

He looked at the translator and then at me and said, "Religion... There are many religions, dear boy, but very little happiness. It suffices that they permitted the slaughter and eating of beasts and birds."

"So then what can I do?" the Basha asked.

"You must acknowledge this living being who has come into the world through you. This will allow you to feel that you will continue on even after your death. There is nothing like a son to give a man the feeling of immortality before he passes away."

The Basha's color changed. "And if I do not acknowledge him?"

After a silent pause, he answered, "The path of denying him is open, but it is bloody."

I felt the Basha was gasping, but without inhaling or exhaling. "How so, wise sir? I don't understand!"

Al-Hakim looked at the translator, then at the Basha and said with anguish, "One of you will perish on that path. Someone's blood will be spilled."

"You seem to be certain of the existence of a son. I am greatly troubled, sir! Why should I acknowledge him if I am going to die at his hands?" the Basha asked again, in the tone of a complaint.

"He will be an extension of you in this world, he and his descendants, even if he kills you. It doesn't matter how you die;

death will inevitably come to you in this final third of your life. What matters is that your blood will continue to pulse through someone's veins on this earth after your own body vanishes."

As if suddenly remembering something important, the Basha asked, "But can you explain to me the coincidence that brought Uroub to my sixtieth birthday party?"

Al-Hakim raised his head with a sigh. "Nothing happens by coincidence. All of it happens in accordance with destiny's will, which led Uroub to you so that you would be led to me. The most unusual thing about you all is your belief in coincidence!"

The Basha pursued his questioning with a tone that made me feel his whole being was foundering. "Will I meet this illegitimate son of mine, if he does indeed exist? And supposing I find him and I acknowledge him, will that change my fate and allow me to live?"

At that point Al-Hakim looked to the translator, then to the Basha, and said, "I have answered all of your questions. I have nothing more to add."

The translator stood up and the usher came in, leaning on his staff. They motioned to us that the meeting was over.

We left the sage's abode dumbfounded by what we had seen and heard. Our shock increased further when we found ourselves not having to bend down the way we had to on our way in. The entrance door was more than two meters high on our way out. As for the cold fire the old man was bathing the snake in, it was now mint green in color.

On the way back, the Basha said, "If what Uroub and Al-Hakim said about my demise is true, then acknowledging my son will not change anything."

From that I understood immediately what decision he had taken, and what I had to do.

## *Samah Shahadeh*

Fawaz returned from Mumbai. His driver brought him home from the airport. The sun was yearning to set.

Whenever Fawaz returned from his travels I got the feeling something about our life was going to change.

Despite the long hug he gave me, I didn't feel the intimacy I was used to feeling when he came back from a trip. I felt he was merely performing a duty. It was a cold hug and I didn't feel the usual embrace of our souls.

In the days that followed, I noticed he was different. He was much quieter and contemplative. He no longer laughed boisterously. He didn't eat like he did before; he was satisfied with a few greens and he told me he no longer liked meat or chicken. He started spending a lot more time in his office, away from me.

I called Sari's wife, Rasha, who was a nutritionist, to ask her to prepare a vegetarian diet plan with detailed instructions for the cook, on account of Fawaz's sudden switch from eating meat and animal products.

I felt that lurking beneath Fawaz's calm exterior was a deep anxiety about some secret matter. I tried to find out what was worrying him and he told me that the deal with one of the currency trading companies he went to India to settle had fallen through.

Plausible, I thought to myself.

I asked Sari and he gave a similar story. Sari was also different from how he had been before the trip.

Then I remembered what Uroub had said about how all cats look gray at night, and how they all looked the same, too.

Another strange thing was that Sari didn't come to our house for many days, which was unlike him. I called him on my cell phone a number of times and he told me he had some family matter to tend to and that he had asked the Basha to pardon his absence.

I could have sought out his wife and asked her what was going on with Sari, but I didn't. Despite my strong affection for Rasha, I felt that my status made it inappropriate to ask.

It was the first time Sari stayed away from our house for such a long period. Previously he came to the house nearly every day, and was never absent or feigned an illness, or came up with excuses. At 9:10 a.m. almost every morning, he would come to the house and sip his coffee with Fawaz while they discussed and reviewed the day's agenda. They would make phone calls and give directives to the managers and bosses at the various offices and companies connected with our group – the Samah Investment Group.

I didn't like sitting with them, because their talk was of no interest to me. But the daily routine always set my mind at ease, because it meant there was nothing new that might be hidden from me.

Now I felt there was a dark cloud hovering over them.

I think I am the type of person who can be patient, and not because I'm older now. It's just the way I've always been since I was a child.

In the end, I would find out what they had been hiding, if indeed they were hiding something from me.

My father always liked to brag about me in front of family and friends, saying that patience and I shared a special bond, despite my young age. Sometimes he swore I had more patience than he did. I hadn't really thought about that before he mentioned it.

My father's comments might have contributed to the transformation of that description into my specialty. I grew up and coped patiently when illness left my mother bedridden for four years before she finally passed away, God rest her soul. I used to personally supervise the nurse who cared for my mother and changed her bedpan, bathed her, and washed her face and her arms. I fed my mother myself and gave her her medicine every day, without ever tiring.

I patiently stayed home alone with the maid for days on the many occasions when my father traveled, and I was very patient as I completed a degree in English literature. And this was despite not really wanting to pursue an English major, except out of deference to my father who thought I should be proficient in at least one language other than my native Arabic, and know its literature. When I told him that my ability to use and comprehend English was much better than other people's because of all my trips to Europe, he told me that didn't excuse me from studying literature.

It probably never occurred to my father that my choice to major in English literature would lead me to choosing Fawaz, who was a fellow student at the university and graduated two years ahead of me.

In college Fawaz was a very calm and self-assured young man, one of those obscure and introspective types. He never chased after any of the other college girls as far as I could see and didn't employ the obvious tactics other guys liked to use to get girls, like showing off in a new car, or parading around in fancy clothes, or talking about their possessions and the power that their father or mother or family exerted. Fawaz was not like that, and he didn't own a car, either, unlike the guys who were always coming on to me or who acted surprised to run into me by coincidence in the narrow walkways beneath the cypress trees, even though they had secretly been following me.

Fawaz was from an ordinary family with a father who owned a perfume shop in the old downtown area. He lived in the Misdar quarter east of Amman in a modest house, but he was very self-confident.

I like people with a self-confidence that doesn't simply come from money or a family name.

That attracted me at the time, and I felt that unlike the others, he didn't trip over himself trying to get to me. That made me happy, because masculinity to me was much more about being noble and proud than being male.

I started stealing glances at him secretly and felt something drawing me to him. Most likely he noticed my attention, but he never made any move to get close to me, which confused me and only increased my attraction to him.

One day I was leaving campus in my car and I saw him standing about 200 meters away at the gate waiting for a ride. I pulled up beside him in my car and he peered inside the window. I waved to him and he opened the door and got in.

I had never given any of my classmates a ride before that, and despite our having seen each other and run in to each other over the course of two years, it was the first time we ever spoke together all alone and in such close proximity.

He was wearing a white shirt and linen trousers and was carrying what appeared to be a very heavy textbook.

In those days I was bent on wearing tight blue jeans and tucked-in blouses, the kind that made my breasts protrude. I let my bangs grow half way down my forehead and tucked the sides behind my ears.

He politely shook my hand. "Thank you, Samah. You shouldn't have troubled yourself."

I liked how he used my first name directly, without using "Miss" the way others did so pretentiously.

I got right to the point and said, "You arouse my curiosity."

That loosened his tongue. "You've said exactly what I have been unable to say myself, with one slight modification. You stir my curiosity and my admiration at the same time."

I discovered he had been following my journey all along, but without making it known.

I dropped him off at Abdel Nasser Circle in Jabal Husein, as he could get home easily from there, and I headed back to my house, thinking of him the whole time.

It was the first time anyone besides my father and mother had found something special about me.

I believed him when he said, "I kept my distance from you as a way of getting close to you. It was the best way to build a relationship with you — you in particular."

What he said was absolutely correct.

My father saw dimensions to people and things that I didn't see. I felt he was different from other men. He had a way of thinking that bewildered and upset me at the same time, because I couldn't keep up with him.

When he found out about my relationship with Fawaz and I told him about his character, his background and his desire to marry me, he surprised me by saying, "Watch out for poor people."

"What's wrong with poor people, Father?" I said, getting worked up. "Aren't they human beings?"

"What I mean is that rich people have certain interests and possessions; they are greedy. You can satisfy them or silence them by either promoting or threatening their interests. Poor people, on the other hand, require caution, because they do not possess anything they fear losing, and because deep down inside they have an inherent desire to take revenge against something, against the rich maybe. But the decision is yours and I will support it no matter what."

## Sari Abu Amineh

It was difficult for me to carry out the task of finding the woman called Muntaha al-Rayyeh because the Basha didn't know her father or grandfather's names. All he had was her first name and her family name. And all he could guess was that she was around sixty years old now, and he remembered that she worked at the Malco Stock Company, which had been liquidated during the wave of failing investment companies that came after the April protests that broke out all over the country in the 1990s and ended up sweeping away the regime of longstanding Prime Minister Zaid al-Rifai.

But I couldn't come across any records belonging to the company at our headquarters. Even the Basha told me, "That company in particular melted like salt. We don't know what happened to all its records and documents. Figure out some other way to find the woman."

A needle in a haystack.

What made my task even more difficult was not being able to seek the help of any of the Basha's employees. The whole thing was top secret. No one was to have any inkling of anything. And even if I covered things up, it was very difficult for me to ensure the dust wouldn't be stirred up by some new development in the future.

I gave one of my relatives, in whose abilities and connections I had a lot of faith and who could be trusted to keep a secret, the job of finding and investigating the woman called Muntaha al-Rayyeh in the civil records and other sources.

There are people in this world created specifically for those types of tasks. They almost always have big ears and a face the shape of an upside down triangle. My cousin was one of them.

After a few days he brought me a report that stated:

*Seventeen women were identified who carry the name Muntaha al-Rayyeh, or Abu Rayyeh, or Abu Rayyah, with variations among them with respect to the father's name or the grandfather's name.*

*Upon inspection of their respective ages, those who fit the requested age profile were narrowed down to seven females.*

*According to the death records, three of those have departed this life: one in the city of Amman, the second in Irbid, and the third in Madaba.*

*With respect to the places of residence of the four remaining females, one immigrated to the United States and another is living in a nursing home in the Jumruk area east of Amman after being diagnosed with early onset of dementia. Another has been living in Saudi Arabia with her husband for the last seventeen years, and the other lives in Swayleh but took up residence there only recently, because the rent contract in the income tax records was dated March 4, 2010 and contains her address and phone number.*

This now made the task much more complicated. What if the woman in question turned out to be one of the ones who'd died? Or emigrated? Or was stricken with dementia? What if *she* was the one who gave birth to the Basha's illegitimate child?

Oh why did I have to go and prepare that surprise for the Basha and bring him Uroub the fortune-teller the night of his birthday?

## Muntaha al-Rayyeh

It felt like ages had passed since those long ago days.

Two whole months went by after that evening I met Fawaz, and I hadn't heard anything from him.

Maybe he had been impressed by my hard work and willingness to stay late as my boss the Porcupine said, but something inside me kept telling me he had different intentions. He had circled around me and brushed his fingers against the back of my neck.

I began to lose hope. I told myself that he must not have liked me.

I truly wasn't trying to be attractive to Fawaz or anyone else, but it was important to me that men found me attractive. It didn't mean I was going to respond to their advances.

Women understand what I mean.

The day Fawaz saw me, he gave me his office phone number at the Sixth Circle building, but I didn't call him. In those days we didn't have mobile phones that could facilitate forming relationships the way we do now. They were non-existent.

After two months and three days, the Porcupine called me into his office to say, "It's your lucky day. Get ready for a trip."

"A trip to where?"

"To Paris. I gave my approval for you to attend a conference on the trade balance between Europe and the Arab world. You will be doing Mr Fawaz's typing for him. This is a golden opportunity. I told you he never forgets hard workers. But if the other employees find out you are the one going to Paris, they'll go berserk and declare you an enemy."

"They're going to find out sooner or later," I said, but then he went on.

"You will request a ten-day vacation starting the beginning of next month, and I will approve it. Don't forget to bring your passport with you tomorrow to get the visa. And don't tell anyone."

*Don't tell anyone.* This statement worried me.

Hesitantly, I said, "But trips cost money and I don't have any."

He laughed so hard I could see his tongue. "All expenses are taken care of, including a stipend. Just go to the Royal Jordanian Airlines office in Abdali with your passport in hand and they will give you your plane ticket."

At night I started thinking: I have never gone outside the borders of my country, and likewise it has never occurred to me – even in my most optimistic moments – that one day I would go to Paris.

Now here I was being given the opportunity to leave the continent of Asia completely.

I asked myself: Could all this be innocent?

Misgivings began to crowd my mind and my soul: It's not innocent, and the Porcupine told me not to tell anyone.

But I also felt another idea swimming against the current and encouraging me to go forward. And so I said to myself: Let it be.

Then I felt as though this thought process going on inside my head was all just an act to cover up the decision that had already been made and was huddling in the corner of my mind somewhere.

I wanted to give the situation the benefit of the doubt and get past my uncertainty. It occurred to me that I knew myself very well and that no one could force me to do anything I didn't want to do. So why should I lock myself out of the world and pass up an opportunity that may never come around again?

When I told my parents, my mother looked me in the eye and said in a listless tone, "What about the expenses?"

"The company's paying," I answered.

Looking over the top of his prescription glasses, my father asked, "Is it mandatory for you to go?"

"No," I answered. "But it could negatively affect my position at the company if I refuse."

He shook his head and didn't say anything.

My mother appeared to have her suspicions, but she encouraged me, which I found very strange.

The day of my trip, I intentionally left late to Marka Airport, and my father ended up contributing to the delay by taking a long time to find a taxi to take all of us — my father, my mother, and myself — to the airport. This served me well, because when we got there, there wasn't any time for them to pry into the details, or to see who would be accompanying me on the trip. I bid them a rushed goodbye for fear of missing my flight and walked through the little passageway leading to the gate area.

# Samah Shahadeh

Finally, after a sixteen-day absence, Sari came to the house.

I was pretty sure Sari was aware he was indebted to me. It was I, after all, who asked Fawaz to offer him his first job, in the accounting department, which involved calling payments due and following up with the various interested parties among the employees and managers.

I got to know Sari through his wife, Rasha, who worked as a nutritionist at Al-Khalidi Hospital in Amman. Rasha came to my room in the hospital while I was recovering from a surgery I had undergone for a female problem. She was very sweet and cheerful, with a pleasant voice and tranquil fair face with naturally red cheeks. She had chestnut-colored hair cut in a short bob style. She had an excellent ability to carry on a conversation, skillfully switching from one topic to another in a manner that warded off boredom and kept one interested, to the point that I begged her to come back in the evening so she might further lift my spirits.

Rasha told me that her husband worked at an insurance agency but had been let go for refusing to change testimony he made under oath in a case that was tried in court. The case ended up costing the firm 300,000 dinars.

She said Sari had a Bachelor's degree in public administration and had graduated with very good grades. He was a highly capable manager and had a lot of experience, but unfortunately luck had not been on his side.

"You can put him to the test in any manner you wish," she said. "He can do any job you deem suitable for him. He can adapt himself to whatever is asked of him. His language skills are excellent and he has an amiable personality – and I'm not just saying that because he's my husband. That's just how he is."

I wanted to help Rasha, this woman I admired for her light spirit and ease of conversation. I gave her my card and I told Fawaz about Sari.

A few days later Sari had two interviews with directors of a credit management and securities company that we own more than fifty percent of. Their positive recommendations caught Fawaz's attention, so he scheduled an interview with him at his home office.

Sari was around thirty-five years old at the time. Fawaz came to me after the interview and said, "He is smart and has a lot of know-how. You know, I posed a random question to him about how many steps he climbed to get to my office and he immediately answered, 'Five.' I asked him about how many *houris* there are on the water fountain in the garden. 'There are nine,' he said. And about the distance between Swayleh and our house and he answered, 'approximately 18 kilometers.' I asked him about the current national budget and he answered me with precision. I asked about the types of businesses in the country, about various sectors of the economy, about social institutions and their divisions, and so on and so forth, and every time his answers were nearly exact. I asked him to prepare a 250-word report on the status of insurance companies and he completed it in twenty minutes. It was focused and precise. And when I asked him to describe the state of the nation in three words he said, 'That is impossible.'"

Fawaz grabbed hold of Sari after that long interview and offered him a job. Then three years later he promoted him to director of public relations and other duties.

Sari became one of us. He would come to the house, keep the Basha company, and sometimes accompany him on business trips. He was worthy of the trust put in him by Fawaz, who spent three hours of his time every morning at his home office, managing his affairs before heading to work.

I made a point of calling Rasha and thanking her for introducing Sari to us.

My opinion of Sari never wavered. Throughout his fifteen years of service he remained trustworthy and loyal and stayed away from the trivialities and insanities that distract some men.

But now, for the first time since he started working for us, Sari was about to become the focus of my investigation.

## Muntaha al-Rayyeh

I feel a mixture of remorse and regret when I think back on those days.

It turned out my plane ticket to Paris was in first class. I didn't know anything about the difference in seating classes on airplanes, and I preferred to limit my questions so as not to look ignorant in front of everyone.

The smell of the airplane was a combination of suitcases and air freshener.

A blonde hostess ushered me to my seat next to the window. I took off my white jacket and placed it on my lap. She asked me if I needed anything. This was new to me – a pretty, well-dressed young woman catering to my every need. I smiled at her and thanked her and before she left me Fawaz arrived and sat down in the seat beside me. He extended his hand politely, so I shook it cheerfully and then busied myself with the contents of my handbag.

When he shook hands with me I noticed his face was almost square and I also noticed the shadow of a heavy beard, despite his having shaved.

"Is this your first trip to Paris?" he asked.

"My first trip on an airplane," I answered, looking directly into his face.

He looked surprised and played with his mustache with his index finger. Then he threw a quick glance at me and said, "Are you afraid of flying?"

He seemed to want to distract me, and a distraction was just what I needed anyway.

But despite the warm tone of his voice, some pauses in our conversation cropped up from time to time. I figured the best way to overcome my discomfort and doubts would be to keep talking and listening.

I told him I didn't know Paris at all and was going to feel out of place there, to which he responded, "I'll be with you. I won't leave you by yourself."

During the flight to Paris he managed to calm me down with his words and his actions, which were not forward or reckless in any way.

When the plane landed at Charles De Gaulle Airport, he reached over and picked up my jacket. "Paris is cold," he said. "You need to put this on."

The way he said "need to" was kind but authoritative, too.

Then he stood up, ducking down, and held the jacket in a manner indicating I should get up and turn around so he could put it on for me, and so I did. He put the jacket over my shoulders and allowed me to do the rest.

At the airport – where a person can easily get lost with all the corridors and gates and escalators – there was a short, blond driver waiting for us wearing a black hat. He picked up our suitcases with enthusiasm and took them to an older model shiny black car. We followed him and sat together in the back seat.

On the way Fawaz said to me, "The hotel we are staying in is near the famous Eiffel Tower."

"I have seen lots of pictures of it. This will be a chance to see it up close."

He looked encouragingly into my eyes. "You can climb the steps, too, if you like."

At the hotel they took me to room 901. He told me he was in room 803.

We parted ways in the elevator. As he was leaving to go to his room he said, "Take a shower and rest up from traveling. We'll join up this evening."

"Take a shower." He said that without the least bit of hesitation. I, on the other hand, was taken aback, as it conjured the image of me standing in the shower naked and wet.

I locked the door behind me and started taking mental inventory of the contents of the room: the comfortable brass bed, the luxurious bathroom with the magnifying mirrors, the two secluded sofas over in the corner, the bowl of fresh fruit on the center table, the yellow flowers in blue vases, the white robe, the towels, the little bottles of shampoo and perfume . . .

I flopped down on the bed and let out a sigh of joy and liberation. I felt life was not without a certain degree of happiness and relaxation. I thrust my hand into the air and got up to get a look at the balcony. I saw women and men swimming freely in a pool of sky-blue water, and lounging on long white chairs.

I thought to myself: I have a hidden and uncharted body. I have never shown it in public before. No man has ever seen it. Why don't I take advantage of my presence here in this foreign country, at this huge swimming pool, and show my body off in front of these people?

I thought: I am not a good swimmer, true, but I could just dip in the water and then lie down on one of the lounge chairs beside the pool. But I have to do it at a time when Fawaz is away from the hotel, so he won't see my body.

In those days, my thought process was more like a jumble of noise in my head accompanied by ready-made decisions that welled up from some obscure place in my brain, unannounced to me and indistinct.

In the evening, my hotel phone rang, startling me. Phones had very loud metallic bells in those days. I picked up the receiver and heard Fawaz's voice. "Good evening, Muntaha. We will go have dinner together. Are you ready?" He said it very politely.

We left the hotel. The driver took us to a restaurant with an ornate entrance gate and stone benches surrounded by decorative plants and statues.

We sat at a round table. He ordered some kind of drink for himself and told me about a women's drink, but I told him I didn't partake of such things. He smiled and said, "I'm talking about a kind of drink that makes women feel happy but won't affect your faculties at all. Give it a try. I take full responsibility."

Then he asked the waiter who was wearing a jacket with coattails to bring me a glass.

If my memory serves me, the drink was red, the color of jujube.

He made a point not to eat or drink before I did. He kept encouraging me to eat. From time to time he would reach over and pick up one of the plates of appetizers, explain to me a little what it was, and then offer it to me, suggesting I try it. As for the drink, he didn't push me to drink too much of it.

He enveloped me with all his attention and attempts to feed me. It wasn't the food itself, but rather the way he was feeding me according to a kind of ritual that consisted of little advances and light touches that appeared to be unintentional.

"When we get back to Amman," he said, "we will stay in touch. I am going to transfer you to a better job. Your current position is no longer suitable for you. You deserve much better."

Fidgeting a bit, I said to him, "That is not important. What matters is that we stay in touch."

The taste of that drink was like a mixture of fruit and some strange flavor that sent me off into the distance.

I don't know what happened that night. I didn't lose my focus one bit, but I felt the world was not a serious place, or at least didn't deserve all the seriousness people attributed to it. I stopped being so cautious with my actions, doing things like crossing my left leg over my right, letting my thigh show from under my green skirt, and responding to his nice stories and jokes. I sensed the foolishness of modesty and social conventions and anything else designed to impede my happiness at that moment.

The gaps in our conversation vanished and I felt as though life was beautiful and damned at the same time.

The waiter came and brought Fawaz a second drink. When he turned to me to ask if I wanted another, Fawaz spoke for me, shaking his head in refusal.

That gesture made me feel his guardianship over me in that foreign land, which was very reassuring.

After dinner he suggested we walk along the streets of Paris, and put my jacket on for me. He was brimming with affection and intimacy as he put my jacket on.

We strolled along streets and through squares. The Paris air was pleasant and refreshing. I saw men and women unabashedly kissing each other in public, and some of the men were fondling their girlfriends' breasts and thighs against walls or lampposts. I felt aroused.

We laughed a lot and put our arms around each other. I felt his warmth and the sweetness of being so close to him. I thanked God I was on a different continent from the one where I lived and where all my relatives and acquaintances lived.

I caught him looking down my jacket and my yellow blouse to get a peek at my cleavage. I had noticed men looking at that intimate part of my chest before, to the point that I had come to the conclusion that these types of glances were an innate reflex of men's eyes. However, Fawaz's look was suggestive of something further.

We got back to the hotel and he walked me to my room. I was in a highly stimulated state and was feeling receptive to life, to people, to everything.

I remember I went inside my room and left the door ajar; then I settled into an upholstered chair beside the bed.

He locked the door behind him and I felt an itch on the bottom of my foot.

He came toward me, his eyes at my knees. He removed his jacket and hung it on a hanger in the closet. His white shirt had a yellow tint from the lamp beside the bed.

## Samah Shahadeh

My curiosity was aroused once again.

I had always been capable of quieting my soul whenever fear and apprehension rifled through it, but this time I couldn't stop it from rebelling in the face of a vague and undefined danger.

If the danger had been clear and well defined, finding a way to deal with it or overcome it would have been easy. That was what I thought about in response to knowing something was being hidden from me.

Anyway, I waited a few more days and then decided to get some information out of Uroub. I used the international phone number I had gotten from her when we met.

She picked up the phone and before I had a chance to say anything, her voice came through, in that Moroccan accent of hers, "Hello, Mrs Samah. So nice to hear from you."

How did she know it was me? I never gave her my phone number that night when we met.

At any rate, nothing was far-fetched when it came to fortune-tellers.

I asked her what she had said to the Basha when she read his palms, and she surprised me by saying, "In my profession, Mrs Samah, there are secrets I never divulge, and that applies to your secrets as well."

Despite being mad at her for not answering my question, I respected that practice of hers, which puzzled me even more, not because she didn't tell me the details of Fawaz's palm reading, but because she actually kept secrets. That was the last thing I expected from a fortune-teller.

But it also meant that what she had told Fawaz was something that had to be kept secret. If it had been just some ordinary thing, she would have told me.

Sari was my only chance now. He had to tell me something.

I hesitated a while, but then I picked up the phone and called Sari's wife. "How has Sari been since getting back from India?" I asked her.

She answered in her usual entertaining manner, "Like someone who's lost a million dinars! Busy, busy all the time. I swear. I tried to find out why, but didn't get anywhere.

"I started wondering if maybe they gave him some kind of secret-keeping herbs over in India. Everything is possible over there. Sari told me that when he went with the Basha to visit an Indian sage there, he saw a man bathing a snake in fire, and the fire was green and didn't burn. What did the Basha tell you about it?"

I was still stuck on the information that Fawaz and Sari had gone to see a sage in India. I asked her what the reason was for going to see him and she said, "God knows. I told you, the Indians flipped Sari upside down."

Annoyed, I said, "Something has gotten into Sari that I don't like."

I loved Sari and Rasha. I loved all my acquaintances. The advice my father had given me – may God give him long life – was still stuck in my memory. "People know who loves them and who hates them from their eyes, their lips, their faces, from what they say and the way they smile and laugh. Love and hate cannot be concealed."

My father's words made me feel I was exposed to others, like I had no way to hide my feelings towards them. So I decided it was safer to show love.

I think people who have gotten to know me know I love them.

But what prompted this anecdote now?

What brought it up was when Rasha said, "It seems like you hate Sari now."

## *Muntaha al-Rayyeh*

I was willing to go on that adventure with Fawaz. Something was pushing me to stay the course with him, to the very end. Until that moment, no man had ever touched me or gotten me alone. So often had I gazed at my body in the mirror, wondering if it would appeal to men up close, or whether I had been fooling myself thinking it was beautiful and exciting. I even heard myself one time saying out loud while looking in the mirror, "Take care of your body before it spoils."

The sounds came out of my mouth without any thought or planning. That same thing happened again in the hotel room. I found myself clinging to myself, then distancing myself from myself, then clinging again.

He sat down beside me and put his hand on my arm and then my chest, so I pushed it back in protest as I looked straight into his face. His forehead was glistening, and his cheeks too, and I could smell the masculine scent of his body so close up. It was a mixture of smells – cologne and skin and alcohol and sweat.

He continued stroking my arm and brought his face close to my neck, so I resisted and refused, not because I didn't want him, but because something inside me kept urging me to refuse. It seemed my resistance made him more and more excited. He put his mouth on my neck and licked it with his tongue. A delightful shiver rushed through my body, and then he picked me up. I felt I wasn't concerned about anything anymore. Someone other than myself had taken over my body, picked it up and laid it down on the bed. He began touching me all over with the palms of his hands and kissing my neck, tickling me with his mustache.

"But you are married!" I said to him, to which he answered, with a voice that seemed to come out from his belly, "Everyone is married. What's the problem?"

I allowed his fingers to ravish my body, now that I was overcome with a desire to have my entire body squeezed.

Yes, I wanted him to squeeze me in his hands like a lemon. I had spent my entire life up to that point without reaping a thing, and now my femininity was insisting that this was the night.

The hair on his chest was very thick and his breath was fiery hot. The throbbing masculinity of his body was transmitted to every bit of my body.

I was no longer capable of holding on to the Muntaha I had known since birth. She had gone down a path of no return and now my body was in the custody of a man, so let him do with it whatever he pleased.

He was sweet and intimate. He honey-coated for me the thorns of my surrender to him. His soothing words perked up my spirit, which had descended from the heights all the way down onto the bed. But I felt a battle breaking out inside me again, between my agitated desires and what I knew about virtue and being wary of men. A silent argument against the concept of virtue took root in my mind and began to grow. It gelled into a silent question I found myself confronting at that moment, which was: Who says the decision to surrender to a man is up to the woman?

That night Fawaz took my virginity with headlong determination. I was surprised no blood dripped from my vagina. Maybe he thought I wasn't a virgin.

He climbed onto me as if he were riding a bicycle, something he repeated numerous times over the course of the next six nights. He even left a meeting scheduled at ten o'clock in the morning to come to my room with a feverish desire, and I was no less desirous, to the point that I left deep scratches in his back with my fingernails.

He bought me an expensive dress and a gold necklace with a Virgo pendant, my astrological sign. And he also put 1,000 dollars in my bag without my knowledge. When I saw it I got really mad. I waited for him to return from a meeting and when he entered my room I threw the wad of bills onto the floor and screamed, "I am not a whore you have to pay to sleep with!"

I started to cry. I didn't know why my crying transformed into a bout of sobbing that went on and on despite his attempts to calm me down. They were more like attempts to pacify me than to satisfy me. He told me the money was merely compensation for the dedication he observed the day he passed by the company building and found me working there all alone long after the other employees had left. He explained that this was his way of rewarding dedicated workers.

As he spoke, he moved close to me, wiped my tears with the palms of his hands, and patted my disheveled hair back into place. I found myself quieting down after my crying fit, and so he went about his quiet invasion of my body once again.

This time I noticed that the back of his shoulders were very hairy.

I knew that what he told me was unconvincing, but there was no turning him away after all that had transpired before that night. I surrendered to him and let him do to me what he pleased, but I insisted on returning his money to him.

Everything else about that week was fun and enjoyable except for one thing, which was that Fawaz could not hold himself back during the final moments of intercourse. And it was in those moments that he took utter control of my body and my soul, becoming like a wild beast that nothing could restrain.

And that is what led to the chain of events that followed and that I did not foresee.

## Sari Abu Amineh

"What you've supplied me with is not enough. I need more detailed information. I need results that I can use," I told the cousin I'd put in charge of investigating Muntaha al-Rayyeh.

He went away for five days and then brought me a new report with several attachments, and it was this report that gave me what I needed:

*Muntaha Rasim Salah al-Rayyeh – the only one who could possibly be the woman in question. She is close to sixty years old and resides in Swayleh, north of Amman. She moved out of her parents' home to a nearby house when she got married. Then she moved to another house in close proximity to that one, which she rented, a distance of three side streets away from the main circle exit heading northeast.*

*According to the marriage records, on December 26, 1982, Muntaha was married to a man by the name of Nael Shakir Yassin Dughaybil.*

*Research into birth records in the months following the marriage revealed that on July 29, 1983, Muntaha and her husband Nael Dughaybil were blessed with the birth of a son, who they named Walid.*

*Research into the registry of students passing the national Baccalaureate exam confirmed that in 2002, their son Walid graduated from Firas al-Ajlouni High School with a grade point average of 98.2. He then attended the Jordanian University, majoring in Shari'a Law, with an academic excellence scholarship funded by the Royal Court, but only completed three semesters before dropping out of school for reasons unknown to the university administration. He left the country after that, via the Mudawwara border crossing, on June 12, 2003, heading for Saudi Arabia to perform the Umrah pilgrimage. However, there is no record in the border registries or airport logs indicating his reentry into the country since that time.*

*Attachments:*
*—ID photos of Muntaha and her husband Nael and their son Walid, according to the data contained in the registers of the Department of Passport Control.*
*—Photocopy of Muntaha and Nael's marriage license, dated 1982.*

What interested me most of all out of the information in the documents my cousin supplied me with was Walid's photo, which I had enlarged so I could examine it carefully. The photo revealed an uncanny resemblance between Walid and the Basha, be it in the protruding sides of the head, the broadness of the forehead, the brown eye color, the thick eyebrows, the curvature of the nose, the color of the skin, or the square shape of the face.

The situation was perfectly clear now. My target was Walid, and the woman we had been looking for was Muntaha Rasim Salah al-Rayyeh. May God forgive me, and her, and her son, and the Basha.

## Muntaha al-Rayyeh

In those days, my mother was suffering from a nightmare called the spinsterhood of her daughter who had reached the age of thirty without getting married. She would rest her chin on her hand and gaze silently at me; I knew she was thinking about me.

As far as I was concerned, it really was not such a big deal. I had refused marriage proposals that started coming my way the moment I turned twenty. That was due to the fact that the men who came to propose weren't what I had hoped for. One was uneducated, another was repulsive with a face that, I'll just say, didn't bring one comfort, and he had fidgety eyes, too. A third didn't have the money to marry me and was planning to take out a loan, a fourth was shorter than me and fat, and number five was forty-five years old at the time.

Nevertheless, I felt that marriage would not pass me by, even if it was to be a little late in coming. I was at peace with that feeling.

However, once I hit age thirty, my mother appointed a friend of hers who lived in Ayn al-Basha, near Swayleh, to be in charge of finding someone to marry me.

That woman's name was Umm Ayyash. I had seen her before. She was a fat woman who was constantly perspiring and had a tattoo under her lower lip.

When I returned from Paris, my parents were waiting for me at the airport.

Once we finished with all the questioning, answering, describing and relaying of the fabricated recap of the conference, none of whose panels or meetings I attended, my mother blurted out, with the excitement of someone sharing some rare and amazing news, "My friend Umm Ayyash came to visit me while you were away, with a groom!"

"Give me a chance to rest first!" I answered.

I needed to know what the future held for my relationship with Fawaz, who said to me as we bid farewell at the entry gate in the airport, "We'll stay in touch."

It was true that I felt – after he made love to me for the last time at the hotel – the presence of a cosmic distance between us, even in those moments when we were joined as one. But I interpreted what he said about staying in touch as an introduction to a relationship that might develop over time.

The day after I got back from Paris, my mother kept eyeing me, and sometimes she would come very close acting like she wanted to hug me, but sniffed me instead, as if she was searching for something inside my body. I was very careful in her presence to act calm and submissive. Then out of the blue she let out a sigh and said, "Your cheeks are red as apples. All from Paris?"

"A single day in Paris is better than a whole year in Swayleh," I answered.

I knew my mother well. She was neither satisfied nor convinced, and she was the type of person who chose her words very carefully, provided she wasn't upset. Sometimes I felt she spoke words of wisdom.

My father didn't care. He just continued treating me with his usual sweetness. At any rate, he was the type of person who gave the benefit of the doubt ten times before drawing a negative conclusion. My mother, on the other hand, doubted ten times before drawing a positive conclusion.

An entire week passed and Fawaz didn't call. I tried to call him but was told he wasn't there. On my final attempt, someone answered who seemed to be very busy.

"My name is Muntaha. I work at the Malco Company, and I would like to speak to Mr Fawaz, please," I said.

"Yes, I know who you are," he answered. "You called two days ago. I told him and he said for you to contact your manager concerning any and all matters."

I was shocked. After a few moments of silence, I said, "Are you sure?"

"Of course I'm sure," he said.

I wasn't expecting Fawaz to marry me or anything, but I did expect us to stay in touch as he had said in Paris, and for us to meet. But for him to end the relationship in this abusive manner?

I scolded myself for what had happened in Paris. How could I have allowed him to do all those things to me?

I was not naïve. But his masculinity had swept me away to a place full of sins. The matter was not in my hands; it was God's fate and divine decree. Yes, God's fate and divine decree.

I could accept using the word "whore" to describe myself during that trip, but I could never accept "naïve."

A thousand times a whore, but naïve, never.

I asked the Porcupine about Fawaz once, shyly, and he answered somewhat sarcastically, looking me directly in the eye, "Why are nightingales not allowed to live in lofty trees . . ."[i]

He didn't finish the line of poetry; instead he stiffened up and said with a scowl, "Mr Fawaz doesn't keep up his relationships. People who become acquainted with him think he has become their friend, but the truth is he forgets about them the moment they finish serving his purpose."

Then he turned his head towards the window and said, "Pay attention to your work and forget about what happened in Paris."

So I had finished serving my purpose, and now the Porcupine mistrusted me, hated me, despised me.

I felt nauseated. My head was spinning. I went back home and buried myself in my bed. My mother followed after me and wanted to know what was wrong. "Let me rest," I said. "I've had a very tiring day."

I locked my bedroom door. My pulse was racing. I was perspiring all over. I wished I would die, truly die. I stayed in bed for days without being sick. I wanted nothing but to bury myself under the covers and be alone.

And that is how my relationship with Fawaz al-Shardah came to an end. I continued feeling the pain of that abuse forever after; I could never forget it.

Umm Ayyash came to our house with a forty-year-old man named Nael — olive complexion, medium height, short brown hair, honey-brown eyes. When he walked, he trotted along and bobbed his head left and right. He had worked as a teacher in the Emirates for eighteen years before settling down in Amman where he opened a clothing store on the main street in Swayleh, near the mosque. He was making a comfortable living, according to Umm Ayyash, but he wanted me to devote myself to the home, not because he was religious at that point, but because he was against women working, according to what she said.

I remembered the Porcupine's insults, and his protruding ears and thin lips. I remembered Fawaz and the way he tossed me aside once he'd taken what he wanted from me. And so I accepted the marriage proposal.

Nael drew up the marriage contract in a matter of days. I felt a sense of relief when I resigned from my post; at least I was free of all the glares from the Porcupine and my co-workers who had found out about my trip to Paris.

A few days before the wedding reception, I began losing my appetite. I started feeling sleepy much more than before and also felt an aversion to certain things.

My mother told me all of that would go away as soon as the wedding was over. She very emphatically explained this was common among girls who were afraid of getting married and topped off her speech by saying, "They're called 'spoiled little girls.'"

After a few weeks, I found myself in the marital bedroom with Nael. He was in such a hurry to penetrate me he almost foiled my scheme to pour a little bit of blood on the white bed sheet.

I discovered four things about Nael that I hadn't noticed at first. First, he was stingy; second, he was truthful and never lied; third, he was voracious in bed, never resting or letting me rest, as if he'd been bottling it up for a thousand years; and fourth, he adored talking dirty during intercourse.

At first I resisted that voraciousness of his, which was painful and exhausted me no end, but eventually it transformed into just a normal part of our lovemaking ritual.

I also saw in him the perfect example of a cuckolded husband who knew nothing of his wife's past. But then I chided myself for thinking such a mean thing.

I cannot say that I loved him, but I didn't hate him. I accepted him as my husband.

I expected his marrying me would put an end to my horror story with Fawaz and would erase all traces of him from my body and my mind, but as it turned out, about a month after getting married, I discovered that the story was about to start all over again, but this time in a different way.

## Samah Shahadeh

Uroub told me, "The important thing is, the cat came back to life."

She also said, "You will discover a secret that has been kept hidden from you for many years, and it will have a major effect on your life in the future."

These were not riddles or cryptic messages. Wasn't it possible Fawaz was married to some other woman without my knowledge?

There really wasn't anything to indicate that was the case, though. Marriage was not a trivial matter. It had certain demands and distinguishing features; it was impossible to hide.

Then was he on the verge of marrying another woman now? So he could have children, maybe?

But he always said he didn't care about having children. He said they eventually just grow up to be scoundrels.

I didn't find out about this side of Fawaz until after we knew for sure that I could not have children. Ever since then he made me feel he hated children. He called them despicable and evil sometimes and talked about them with such animosity I could hardly take it.

One evening he said to me, "You watch a lot of Hollywood movies. Haven't you noticed that in some horror movies they use children's voices in the background to make the scenes extra scary?"

That Fawaz had a second wife was more likely to be the case, even if I had my doubts. Uroub did say that the secret had been hidden from me for a long time.

It was something that had happened in the past, not something that was going to happen in the future. Big difference.

Sari's wife came over to review Fawaz's vegetarian diet plan. "I need you to do something for me," I said to her.

"As long as you don't ask me to find out what secret Sari is hiding. He's like a black box, receives but doesn't transmit. Even when his cell phone rings, he steps into another room, locks the door, and keeps his voice down so I can't hear. I need one of those devices they put in walls or doors so I can spy on him."

"Good idea. Why don't you do that?" I said.

Rasha was quiet for a minute and then said, "Do you think I'm capable of such a thing, Mrs Samah?"

Rasha respected herself and loved her husband, and she always made sure to treat me with a level of respect that endeared her to me – unlike so many of Fawaz's friends' wives or the wives of managers and executives of his companies and offices.

It was a relationship free of the kind of bootlicking and deception I couldn't stand.

Naturally, Rasha never brought her two children with her when she came to visit, even though they weren't little anymore. Sari understood Fawaz's aversion to children and adolescents.

For me, my feelings towards children were directly related to how clean, quiet, and mild-tempered they were.

I didn't know if Fawaz's position towards children would have been different if I'd borne him a son or a daughter.

## Muntaha al-Rayyeh

I know I am better versed on the topics of misery and despair than of happiness, and the reason for that is known to me at least.

In the days following my marriage I started feeling increasingly nauseated and there were other changes in my body that I didn't understand. I started vomiting and going to the bathroom a lot. I lost my appetite and started having cravings for things that had never crossed my mind before – ice cubes, chalk, cumin – and I would often lick the walls with my tongue. Every time I looked in the mirror my face looked paler.

I thought my worst fears had come true because of what Fawaz did to me, so I kept it to myself and didn't let Nael see any of the symptoms. Then I went to the doctor without Nael's knowledge. When the doctor got the test results back, he exclaimed like a herald of glad tidings, "Congratulations! Your fetus is in its ninth week!"

I remembered Fawaz, and I knew the baby was his. I couldn't decide what to do and didn't know who to turn to for help other than my mother.

I went to see her and told her everything. She slapped her cheeks with the palms of her hands three times. Then she let out a shriek and spat in my face. "Abort it, you bitch!"

I wiped my face with a napkin and said, appealing to her devoutness, "But isn't that *haram*?"

"And what you did with that bastard in France," she screamed, "wasn't that *haram*? I swear if you had told me before you married

Nael, I would have cursed that bastard and his whole family! I would have dragged him through the courts and made him pay up and down for what he did!"

"So I should repay the sin with another sin?" I said.

"Shut up, you whore!" she screamed. "Whores are the last people who should talk about *halal* and *haram*!"

I shut my mouth. She went back to hitting the palms of her hands together. "If Nael finds out," she said, "he will divorce you."

"That might be for the best," I said. "He is very stingy, actually."

Of course my father didn't know anything about what transpired between my mother and me. I think fathers are the very last to know about such matters, if they ever find out at all.

My mother took me to see a gynecologist she knew, to perform the abortion for me. She was a doctor with blonde hair – a little too blonde, really, and on top of that, she refused, saying it was against the law and she would get in trouble if she did it.

We went to a male doctor that we didn't know, and he also refused. He said it was *haram*.

The situation grew complicated, but my mother kept looking for a solution. Then two days later, she raised her eyes to the heavens praising God and said to me, "Listen, you whore. According to the doctor, you will give birth in less than seven months, because by then the fetus will have completed nine months. You have no choice but to refuse to have the baby in the hospital and ask instead for the registered midwife to attend the birth. Then leave the rest to me. I will make her let your husband think his son has been born prematurely."

"Do you think such a plan could work?" I asked.

"It worked for a woman I know," she piped up, "a woman the likes of you. And don't forget your husband is stingy and midwife fees are nothing compared to the hospital."

I felt as though God was truly sublime in His wisdom. He created premature babies in order to protect the likes of women like me.

I began thinking about how another being other than myself existed inside me, a being that would develop and grow.

What kind of blood would circulate through its veins?

## *Sari Abu Amineh*

Never before in my life had I felt such anguish and anxiety as I did now.

Mrs Samah wanted to know what Uroub had told the Basha.

Most importantly, Mrs Samah was the daughter of Nayef Shahadeh, the grand Basha, the shrewd gentleman she introduced me to as we were leaving the Sheraton Hotel ballroom after a classical musical performance by a Greek musician invited by one of the princes.

I had taken my wife, Rasha, to the concert, in the company of Fawaz Basha and Mrs Samah. There we met Nayef Shahadeh – a man with thin white hair and a fair complexion speckled with brown age spots. He had cold blue eyes, but they were cunning, too, I thought. He was slim and neatly attired and had an air of determination and tranquil reverence.

He was wearing a navy blue suit with a subtle pattern of tiny white dots, over a pure white shirt whose starkness was broken by a sea-blue necktie. It was a perfect display of an older gentleman dressed with lavish elegance.

Despite her father's involvement with so many people who wanted to shake his hand and stand close to him, Mrs Samah grabbed my wife by the hand and said to both of us, "Come let me introduce you to my father."

Fawaz Basha was also wrapped up with hand shakers and people wanting to stand with him.

Mrs Samah walked ahead of us, without letting go of Rasha's hand, and went right up to him, right through the crowd of people surrounding him, and introduced us. Pointing to Rasha, she said, "This is the beautiful Rasha, Mr Sari's wife."

He bent forward respectfully and kissed her hand. The crowd withdrew, leaving us alone with him – Mrs Samah, Rasha, and I.

The man was roughly eighty-five years old.

Then Mrs Samah pointed to me and said, "Sari is the man I told you about."

He greeted me with captivating kindness and we shook hands. His hand was very soft. Then a bald man who had been standing nearby approached us and handed me a business card with Nayef Shahadeh's name and phone number on it.

Rasha was the height of elegance in her wine-colored dress with slits in the shoulders and sleeves. That dress perfectly complemented her figure and skin tone and her hair, which was very long in those days.

But what was I to do about Mrs Samah and what she wanted to know about the Basha? Did I have it in me to let myself squander the Basha's secrets? And to whom? His wife?

Sometimes I felt the presence of a thing in my life called 'bad luck'. A kind of lurking unluckiness that lay in wait, ready to pounce on me at just the right moment. That happened to me while I was at the insurance company, before I started working with the Basha. Another time my son, Suhayl, fell off the wall near our house in Um Uthaina and broke his leg just hours before I took off on a trip to Milan with the Basha. And when I got back, my wife informed me the doctors had discovered she had breast cancer, which made me worry about her incessantly while I looked after her throughout her chemotherapy treatments until she made a full recovery.

If Mrs Samah were to find out what Uroub said, she would turn the world upside down. At least that's what I thought.

As for the grand Basha, if Nayef Shahadeh were to find out, only God knew what would happen.

That was a very frightening possibility indeed – for Mrs Samah and her father to find out that the Basha had had an affair with another woman, and had fathered a child with her, all this while she sat happily at home living the kind of peaceful life that would be difficult for any other woman to achieve.

I didn't think the fact it had been so many years since the Basha had the affair would necessarily work in his favor, and I knew Mrs Samah would never allow herself to be the last to know. She seemed quite determined to find out the truth.

In the end, as long as she was searching for it, it was inevitable she would eventually stumble upon the truth. That was a principle I had complete faith in.

True she was a refined and proud woman, but these kinds of situations were considered to have crossed the boundaries of refinement, tolerance, and pride.

"OK," she said to me. "What is it that is worrying the Basha so much and causing him to wake up several times a night, every night?"

"You are closer to him than I am, ma'am."

She scowled and said, "But this only started happening after your trip to India."

"You're right," I said in a comforting tone. "But I don't have an explanation."

She stared at me a long time. "I hope for your sake that what you're saying is true." Then she gave me a scornful look and said, "How beautiful and peaceful life was before Uroub showed up!"

## Muntaha al-Rayyeh

My mother's plan worked. Nael was overjoyed by the birth of what he believed was his baby boy, two months premature. He obtained a birth certificate for him under the name Walid Nael Shakir Dughaybil using the stamped official document provided to him by the midwife, who took care of Walid at our house for a week after his birth.

He was always asking me about "*al-Walid,*" "the baby," "*the Walid.*" He would say, "Where is *al-Walid*?" and "How is *al-Walid*?" It got to the point where I even started calling him "*al-Walid*" instead of just "Walid."

Nael came to be known as "Abu al-Walid," and he loved to dote on him in a high-pitched voice while I held him in my lap. He made whistling noises with his mouth that sounded like a bird chirping.

As the months passed, I noticed al-Walid bore a strong resemblance to Fawaz. I started lying to Nael, saying things like, "He has your forehead, and your face and neck, too."

That made him so happy I started feeling sorry for him. When al-Walid turned one year old, Nael said to me in front of my mother, "His forehead doesn't look like mine, and neither does his face."

My mother quickly changed the subject. "Children change a lot, but his forehead is an exact replica of my grandfather's, God rest his soul. He resembles you in his eyes and his neck. God is such a wonderworker!"

Two years after we got married, Nael repainted the white walls of the living room a light green color. Within just a few days after that, he became a religious fanatic, even though he had not been religious at all before, and he immersed himself in his work.

He grew a beard and started wearing a short *dishdasha* robe. He also started carrying a *miswak* twig around with him and would take it out and brush his teeth with it from time to time. It disgusted me the way he bared his teeth while brushing them with the *miswak*. His front teeth were brown in color up near his gums. But I didn't say anything to him, because he seemed very excited about his newfound enlightenment and piety. He even re-merchandized his clothing store and started specializing exclusively in Islamic women's dress.

When al-Walid turned seven, Nael started taking him along with him to the mosque. Then he taught him to go on his own and to attend religion classes and whenever al-Walid would tell us about what he heard and learned at the mosque, Nael's face would beam with joy and satisfaction.

It seems Nael felt there was something imperfect about my name, so to avoid it he started calling me "Hajji," even though I had never performed the Hajj. I had been content covering my hair with a scarf and doing modest prayers, like all the other women in our quarter. But that scarf was the source of many a problem with Nael. I didn't like winding it tightly around my head and neck, because it made me feel like I was choking. Whenever he would see my hair sticking out from under the scarf he would blow up in my face and accuse me of harlotry and unveiling and other expressions I can't remember and can't pronounce. Then he swore he would never go out in public with me unless I wore *niqab*.

And in fact, we did not leave the house together after that, and he also started avoiding me, to the point that I felt a vast distance growing between us.

Al-Walid never learned how to lie. He was truthful, just like Nael. And he used to pray for God to protect us and protect our home, especially when he performed the night prayer.

He seemed much older than he actually was. He had a tendency to isolate himself in his bedroom and I would often find him sitting cross-legged submissively on the floor, the Holy Quran in his hands. Whenever I asked him about something during his silent Quran readings, he wouldn't answer, as if he were living in some other place outside our home and my voice didn't reach him.

He read a lot, to the point where he hardly talked to me at all anymore. His room was redolent with a smell that reminded me of the embalming fluids they use on the dead before burying them. The smell bothered me. Numerous times I cleaned his room while he wasn't home, and burned incense, and splashed essence of marjoram to try and get rid of that smell. But it would come back as soon as he reentered the room, as if I hadn't cleaned or fumigated it.

I complained to Nael about him and he sharply retorted, "How can you interrupt him when he is reading holy verses? How can you remove the smell of perfume oil from his room? Don't you know that what you are doing is a sin?"

"But that smell bothers me, Nael," I said.

"Bothers you?" he replied. "Do you know that using perfume oil was a practice of our noble Prophet? And do you know he would rub musk oil into his hair and one could see its sparkle and sheen in the part of his hair?"

Mutual understanding between Nael and al-Walid and me worsened with the passing of the months and years, especially once black hair started sprouting out of al-Walid's chin and under his nose and his voice deepened and he shot up in height.

## Samah Shahadeh

Fawaz started receiving visitors I had never seen before. I happened upon them a number of times while sitting on the second-floor balcony as they were leaving their cars and drivers and entering our house through the garden on their way to Fawaz's office.

They were men dressed in fine suits, seemingly preoccupied with important matters. Their faces were indecipherable. Each time they came they would meet with Fawaz for an hour or more and then leave, with the same faces and same expressions. There were seven of them in total.

I noticed that Sari was always away whenever they came around. In fact, those particular men never met with Sari, at least not at our house.

"How come Sari doesn't join in your meetings with those people?" I asked Fawaz.

He gave me a look of surprise and said, "Are you seriously asking this question? If so, I'd have to say that you are living in one valley and I in another!"

Using this as an opportunity to show him my concern about what was going on with him, I said, "As a matter of fact, we have been living in two different valleys for some time now!"

"Not so much that you should start thinking Sari must accompany my every step," he added.

"But you took him along with you to see the sage in India," I said.

I was expecting to see some kind of reaction in his face or his speech, but he didn't show any evidence of surprise at my knowing that bit of information.

Nothing surprised Fawaz anymore, as if surprise had vanished from his life. As if there was no longer anything in this world that could shock him.

Ever since he returned from India, he had become cold and unexcitable.

I said to myself that either he had reached such heights of understanding that he was immune to excitability because he had seen it all before, or he had been bombarded with so many surprises that he had lost heart and simply could not respond to another one.

Either way, it was unsettling.

"I get the feeling there is something new in your life," I said to him. "At the least, those people never used to come to our house before."

"Not at all," he replied. "Nothing new, Samah."

I sensed he had read between the lines and answered the question hidden in my words.

So what was the secret that had been hidden from me for so long?

On the other hand, why couldn't Uroub be a liar?

Why had I granted her all my trust and believed everything she said?

## Muntaha al-Rayyeh

When al-Walid was almost eighteen, he let his black beard grow, and he was no longer the child I used to take care of. He started avoiding me. He was closer to Nael than to me, and I felt he was like some entity growing and developing, far away from me.

The imam from the mosque started asking for him to read the Holy Quran during Friday prayers and to recite prayers after him. Then he memorized the Quran, and I used to hear him reading verses out loud in his room. He won first place in the Quran memorization contest, and the Religious Endowment Ministry rewarded him generously. But afterwards he just kept to his room, quietly reading verses from the Quran and performing prayers. He quit reciting the Quran in a loud voice like he used to, as if he had hit upon a Quranic interpretation forbidding that practice.

After that, his words and manner of speaking changed.

He started saying, "*As-salaamu 'alaykum,*" (Peace be upon you) rather than "Good morning," or "Good evening." And he began criticizing me for being unveiled, even though he and Nael were the only men in the house. In addition, he started tacking the phrase "*hadaaki Allah,*" (May God guide you on the right path) onto his requests to me. For example, if he said, "Wash my robe," he would tack on, "*hadaaki Allah,*" instead of "please."

Little by little, al-Walid's speech became new to me, and unfamiliar.

When he passed the Tawjihi Baccalaureate Exam, he received the distinguished academic achievement scholarship and began studying Shari'a law at the Jordanian University.

But he would come back home from the university very upset and would complain to his father about the immoral ways of the students – female and male – and their disregard for religion. Then he started meddling in my personal affairs, insisting I wear *niqab* whenever I left the house, and his father backed him up on that. It got to where I felt there was a male opposition front against me.

I said to al-Walid firmly, "I do not want to wear *niqab*, you hear?"

"Our law does not succumb to whims," he replied. "It is the duty of every Muslim man and woman to abide by it."

I claimed I was allergic to *niqab*, that it stifled my ability to breathe. But he insisted and kept repeating that men were the guardians over women, which is the verse I thought pertained only to marriage. I came to find out it applied to all males, even to a woman's son. Likewise I discovered that my relationship with him had been shaken up. He started taking on the role of my preacher or my father rather than my son, and I dodged those sermons the way a daughter dodges such lectures from her father.

The battle over the *niqab* ended in his defeat, because I gathered up all my strength and put him down. I told him that the person who would force me to do what I didn't want to do had yet to be born, and if God created such a person, I would kill him with my own hands before I let him interfere with my life.

And when he shouted at me, I slapped him on the back of the neck three times.

He endured the slaps and said, with his hand on his neck, "May God forgive you, Mother."

That night, I heard him praying to his Lord, loud enough to be heard, for me to be guided onto the right path.

I liked the way he respected me after I slapped him, so I reconciled with him, but he told me he was not upset about what I had done, because respect for one's parents was a foundational tenet of Islam.

A month later, al-Walid and some of his sheikh friends decided to perform the Umrah pilgrimage. And so I asked him whether he would be missing classes as a result.

"Yes," he replied. "I will be absent from the university. Perhaps God will forgive the sins of my studying there."

I made an appeal to Nael, hoping he might step in and persuade him to postpone his Umrah until the summer vacation rather than missing his classes.

"Leave him to his own matters," he replied. "He is a good Muslim, mature and sensible and is aware of what he is doing."

The day he left for the Umrah, he wished me a heartfelt goodbye. He kissed my hand and forehead three times. Nael, on the other hand, accompanied him to the Umrah travel agency building.

Al-Walid has not returned since that time. I discovered that he joined the mujahideen. It was Nael who told me; he was pleased al-Walid went to Afghanistan and showed great pride in the fact that his son had joined the mujahideen. Whenever I remembered him and wept, Nael would say to me, "Say that God is One, Hajji. Al-Walid is a mujahid; he is dear to God. God has blessed me with this faithful son who is devoted to his religion and its tenets. And He has blessed you along with me. We will have our reward with God the Sublime. I swear if I were his age, I would join him in jihad."

With my palm on my cheek, I gazed at Nael and shook my head.

But I never thought and never imagined that a day would come when a man named Sari would come to see me, now that I was in my sixties, and ask me if thirty years ago I had given birth to a son named Walid, whose father was Fawaz al-Shardah, now known as Fawaz al-Basha.

## *Abu Hudhayfah*

His jihadi name was Sharhabil, after the venerable Companion of the Prophet Sharhabil Bin Hassneh, conqueror of Jordan. It was chosen for him by his spiritual comrade Habibullah al-Tunisi a few months before a raid east of Jalalabad in which the mujahideen destroyed a squad of NATO forces who had gotten too close to a secret mujahideen training camp. They managed to kill six of the thirteen NATO troops while only Habibullah al-Tunisi earned martyrdom. He had thrown himself onto the ground pretending to be dead, which caused the remaining foot soldiers to gather around him. That was when he blew himself up and annihilated them, with help and success granted by God, the Exalted, the Majestic.

Sharhabil joined the mujahideen in Jalalabad one year after the American invasion of Afghanistan and was trained in their mountain hideouts. He participated in numerous battles and raids and soon developed a reputation for his exceptional skill at firing anti-tank rocket launchers.

Walid Nael Shakir Dughaybil. That was Sharhabil's real name, which he decided to change when he joined the mujahideen. Habibullah al-Tunisi, may God have mercy on his soul, helped him choose that particular jihadi name, which he liked.

When Sharhabil came to us in Kandahar from Jalalabad, we had barricaded ourselves in one of the craggy mountain hideouts and were lying in wait for the NATO forces. They had been carrying out preemptive strikes on us after finding our hideouts, for fear we would carry out attacks on their camps. We were waiting for them to fall into our trap.

Sharhabil had long hair and a long beard. As for his square face, it appeared very white against all his black hair. I saw in his eyes a kind of radiance that put one at ease at first sight.

He came to us dressed in Afghan garb. Hanging from his right shoulder was a sack made of linen cloth. His sandals had rubber soles, which he made himself out of a tire from one of the NATO vehicles he destroyed in Jalalabad. His body and face showed clear signs of fatigue, but he gave no indication whatsoever that he wanted to rest or sleep. In fact, he asked our squad leader for his jihadi orders.

But instead, our commander, Abu Zubayr, with his long face and shiny bald crown, handed him a *miswak* twig for cleaning his teeth in the coming days, and also some black dates and a bowl of water to provide for his needs and to quench his thirst after his long journey. Then he said to him, "We will talk after you've had some sleep and perform night prayers." Then he looked at me and said, "Abu Hudhayfah, I have entrusted Sharhabil to you so he can see his way through the muddle of our craggy mountain hideouts and trenches."

The sun was sinking into the west behind the lofty mountain, which looked pitch-black and seemed to be warning us of a long dark night ahead. I remembered the sunset behind the hills of my village of Harija in Tihamat Asir. I remembered the chaste wife I bid farewell to after only ten months of marriage in order to answer the call to jihad for the sake of God.

I imagined her in all her virtue and brilliance waiting for me at the gate to our house, bidding farewell to the sunset and traversing the distant roads with her eyes.

May God be with you, my dear wife. How I have missed you, and how miserable my life has been without you. But it is the call to jihad, and I am merely one of God's servants who, ". . . have never changed (their determination) in the least . . ."ii

We were twenty-four mujahideen in the hideout, hunkered down in five trenches that were all connected to each other. Our noses were stuffed up with the smell of dirt and moist earth. Cobwebs clung to our clothes and ants crept inside our clothes to our skin. We armed ourselves with faith and courage and we had an intense longing to reach Paradise, which awaited us, with God's permission.

Sharhabil rested his tired body on an animal skin mat we had seized earlier. I looked into his eyes. His droopy eyelids made it clear that he hadn't slept in a very long time. As was our custom, whenever a new mujahid came to us we vowed to fight if we were attacked by the enemy at night. We wished for each other the great prize of martyrdom and then I left him and returned to my mujahideen brothers to resume keeping watch over our hideout, which we had named "Osama Bin Zayd." It was one of nine hideouts for the Arab mujahideen in that redhot zone, which extended over more than ten kilometers.

## Samah Shahadeh

It was possible that the events in Tunisia, Libya, Iraq, Syria and elsewhere were what was bothering Fawaz.

I knew that his business dealings in those countries had been hurt by the conflicts breaking out in those places. He had to close two of his offices in Libya and a securities investment company branch as well. He also shut down two currency exchange branches he had opened up in Damascus when the Syrian authorities allowed non-Syrians to open up money exchange offices. And as for Baghdad, he told me he would have to close his offices there as well if the bombings continued.

But how could he have not foreseen what was happening in those countries?

Ever since the early days of our marriage, it had always been his uncanny and unique intuition that had led to his great success in the various business ventures he managed and carried out.

He had an intuitive ability to predict disasters and major events before they happened.

After our marriage, which my father unenthusiastically agreed to, I felt my father gradually warmed up to Fawaz. He asked him to think about some projects that would be of benefit to us. It was only three days after the Iraqi invasion of Kuwait when Fawaz finished refurbishing two buildings my father owned in the Um Uthaina area. The buildings had been left unfinished and neglected because of permit issues. Fawaz completed restoring them just before the influx of Palestinians and Jordanians who left Kuwait and headed for Jordan after the Iraqi occupation, and rented them out to them at exorbitant prices.

Likewise, he bought huge sums of Kuwaiti dinars at the time and sold them for many times the rate he had bought them for, after the Iraqi forces pulled out of Kuwait and went back home.

My father, who could read people with his little blue eyes, said to me, "The difference between Fawaz and other entrepreneurs is that he is good at arithmetic."

Then he told me that he had grown to like Fawaz after being skeptical of him at first.

Actually, my father didn't like Fawaz. He did stop being wary of him, though. When I asked him if he had changed his opinion about needing to be careful with poor people, he said, "Not at all. The principle of being wary of the poor still stands. That will never change."

"Are you still wary of Fawaz?" I asked.

His answer surprised me. "No, I am not wary of him at all," he said. "I made him into a rich man after he married you."

My father is still living, may God give him many more years. He lives in his house near the Baccalaureate schools west of Amman, with his maid and his security guard and his driver. He still holds three posts in consulting that don't require any work or regular hours. One is with the Arab League, another is with the Phosphate Company, and the third is with Amman Stock Exchange.

Even though he submitted his resignation from these posts more than once, they came to him at his home each time and persuaded him to withdraw the resignation, because having his name associated with those posts boosted people's confidence.

Fawaz also predicted the invasion of Iraq. He went around making deals buying foods and medicines at discounted prices in order to ship them to Baghdad at international market prices, all in line with the food and drug agreement approved by the United Nations. We reaped formidable profits from that.

He always followed his intuition, and he always responded to his critics' admonitions by saying that the difference between him and them was that he trusted his intuition.

Could his intuition have guided him this time to foresee a new disaster about to happen? Was he contemplating some way to profit from it?

Even if this were the case, he would turn the disaster into a source of increased wealth, not increased obscurity and anxiety and making me anxious along with him!

At least that was how he used to be.

# Abu Hudhayfah

When Sharhabil woke up from his sleep, he recited the *shahada*, asked God's forgiveness, performed ablutions, and stood to perform the night prayer, *qiyam al-layl*.[iii]

When he was finished, I informed him of what the two watchmen had relayed to us about a potential raid by the NATO forces. I asked him to go to our commander, Abu al-Zubayr, in the trench next to ours to apprise him of our orders in the event of an attack.

It soon became clear to me that Sharhabil was different from others who had been sent to us from other hideouts. He didn't ask a lot of questions and didn't make anyone feel he needed them. He was a man of few words and shied away from the kinds of exaggerations many mujahideen engaged in when describing their raids. Similarly, the way he sat and walked and spoke, all gave the impression he was one solid mass.

The first battle he embarked on took place only eight hours after his arrival to our hideout. Our lookouts had informed us from their advanced positions that the NATO troops were preparing for an attack on several of our hideouts, and our commander was expecting them to make a raid on us in a matter of hours. He commanded us to teach them a harsh lesson, with our faith, our courage, our precise aim, and our patience.

Our commander, Abu al-Zubayr, was correct in his prediction. Just as we were performing the dawn prayers, which he decided should be *salat khauf* "fearprayer,"[iv] half of us performed half the number of prescribed prostrations while I stayed with the other half to keep watch, and when they finished they switched to keeping watch while we took our turn performing prostrations with the imam. While Abu al-Zubayr was leading us in prayer, we heard the rumblings of jets. He kept leading us without interruption and he gave no indication we should do anything unlawful out of necessity. When we completed our prayers, he asked God's forgiveness and then prayed for us to earn either victory or martyrdom. Then he broke to us the good news that "Almighty God deigned for this battle to be our fate," and then asked us to renew our pledge and recommit ourselves to each other. And before we finished pledging ourselves to achieving either victory or martyrdom, air fire started raining down on us from the skies in all directions. The sound of bullets ricocheting off the rocks and stone was very sharp and could be heard from where we were in our underground tunnels.

Abu al-Zubayr said, "We must remain under cover and stay alert until the fighter planes finish the round of softening airstrikes they are carrying out in order to clear the way for the entry of armored personnel carriers and ground troops."

The sound of gunfire no longer frightened me the way it did when I first joined the mujahideen. Fear used to grip me ahead of a battle with our enemy, but as soon as the fighting began, the fear would dissipate. After that all I cared about was trying to cause the greatest number of losses to our enemy's ranks.

Before dawn broke, we heard the distant rumble of machines. Our lookouts had informed us they were coming our way and getting close to our hideouts. And so Abu al-Zubayr told us to scatter to different locations – behind the rocks, in holes in the ground, in caves and tunnels – depending on our weaponry. He said to Sharhabil, as he handed him one of the six anti-tank rocket launchers we captured in a previous raid on a group of Afghan soldiers working with the Americans, "On this blessed dawn you will show us your sharpshooting skills and destroy our enemy's machines."

Sharhabil uttered the formula, "*Bismallah al-rahman al-rahim*," (In the name of God, the Beneficent, the Merciful) while puffing air onto his palms, rubbing them together, and then strapping four rockets onto his chest. Then he raised the rocket launcher onto his shoulder and said, "*Wa ma ramayta idh ramayta wa lakinna Allah rama*," (When you threw, it was not your act but God's act[v]). Then he left the tunnel with clear resolve and determination.

Abu al-Zubayr was very tough. His words struck us like lightning whenever we forgot something or fell short. He even forbade us from yawning, which he once told us had something feminine about it and was not becoming of men.

# Sari Abu Amineh

Things did not end with finding Muntaha al-Rayyeh. Next I was asked to meet her and speak with her. I was to find out all there was to know about her son, Walid, plus find out how she got in touch with him: address, telephone number, where he could be found, and whether he had visited her secretly, and if so, when and how?

Could a fortune-teller's predictions really elicit so much attention from the Basha?

My primary concern had been to succeed in giving the Basha a surprise at his birthday party, no matter what the consequences were going to be. At any rate, it hadn't even been my idea. It was something the Grand Basha, Nayef Shahadeh, had concocted and I borrowed the idea because he was going to have to miss the party due to travel. But I never expected things would turn out the way they did, and cause me to lose control of everything.

Maybe Uroub had been able to read between the lines when I spoke to her while driving her from her hotel to Fawaz's house. Maybe she had been able to connect the invisible strings attached to what I was saying and telling her about the Basha. But how could she have come up with the idea that he had an illegitimate son?

As for the part about her prophecy of the Basha's demise coming at the hands of this son of his, I could not banish from my heart the conviction that had sprouted after going with the Basha to see

Harsha al-Hakim, which was that fate was an undeniable truth that must be acknowledged and that Uroub was an extraordinary woman who possibly did not even belong to the humble human race. Likewise I would no longer be able to hold on to my prior belief that fate was merely an ancient myth that preceded religions, a myth that transformed into an accepted truth because of its connection to the unknown.

My wife started to annoy me with her questions and the way she kept looking at me. I found myself having to keep my distance from her whenever my phone rang so she wouldn't hear my conversations. She was very close to Mrs Samah and might tell her what she'd heard me say on the phone.

True, Rasha was extremely devoted and faithful to me and to my home, but she might not be able to resist the pleasure of passing gossip along to Mrs Samah, who I didn't doubt had asked her what was going on with me.

I really started feeling irritated by Rasha. I felt as though the space between us had become highly flammable, could ignite into a flash fire at any moment.

It was the fourth time during our marriage that I'd gotten that feeling.

In the past it had been a gradual feeling that started out obscurely. At first I would be on the lookout for every mistake in her actions and her words. Then I would start analyzing everything she said and finding the hidden meaning behind her words or what they implied. Next, I would look at her in an unkindly manner and start making her feel like she was intentionally trying to harm me when she served me food I didn't like, or when she went to bed early despite the affectionate advances I started making as soon as the sun went down, or when she asked me about matters that were none of her business, or when she went around the house day and night wearing those loose-fitting linen pants that decreased my desire and nearly turned me off completely. All of that would pile up and suddenly I would find myself casting evil glances I couldn't hide. On her end, she would start showing signs of being on her guard and couldn't hide it either. This was the point when the space between us became combustible, and required only the tiniest spark to make it go up in flames.

This time, the spark that ignited a fight between us was our two children, Suhayl and Suhayla. Suhayl, who had reached age sixteen and whose voice had deepened and whose pale white face had broken out in pimples, was always closing himself off in his room and immersing himself in video games and the Internet. He behaved like a hotel guest in our home. And his sister, Suhayla, was approaching puberty with her own confused emotions. She had started being stubborn with her mother and her brother who was two years older than her. She was always disgruntled. Sometimes she would lock herself in her room and wouldn't talk to anyone.

I headed towards the kitchen. Rasha was standing at the sink.

"Why doesn't Suhayl pay more attention to his studies instead of spending all his time on the Internet and playing games on the computer?" I said to her, nervously. "And why has his sister gotten so stubborn?"

Rasha immediately put all the responsibility on me, for not paying enough attention to them, not spending enough time with them and not taking care of them.

"That blessing is yours," I said sharply. "You're the one who spends the most time with them. So why are they acting this way?"

She looked me directly in the eye and said, "I've done what I can, but they have a devious bloodline."

I was furious. I screamed at her and scolded her. I was in a rage and started threatening her and breaking everything I could get my hands on – plates, glasses, pots and pans. Suhayl came running from his room and stood between us, stopping us from swinging at each other.

That fight led to a rift between us that lasted many days. It was useful because I really needed Rasha to stop asking me about the Basha and about what was going on with me. That need fortified me and gave me the ability to persevere while she avoided me and gave me the silent treatment.

She was too smart, however, not to figure out my scheme. She made up with me after four days and immediately went back to questioning me.

That was the first time she had ever been the one to apologize first.

# Muntaha al-Rayyeh

Ten years have passed since al-Walid left.

He contacted me only once, when he found out Nael had died of a brain aneurism. He very casually conveyed his condolences, without shedding a tear. He was cold.

"May God have mercy on his soul," he said. "He was an upright man and carried out his religious duties with loyalty and dedication. But this is God's wisdom and will. May Paradise be his abode, with God's permission."

I asked him how he was doing and he told me he was living the purest moments of his life. Then he fell silent. I thought he must be upset about Nael's death.

"What's wrong, al-Walid?" I asked. "Why don't you say something?"

"I was going to ask you about a certain matter," he said hesitantly.

"What is it?" I said.

"Nothing, Mother," he answered tersely. "Nothing."

He was having difficulty speaking. Maybe he thought my phone was bugged. He didn't extend the conversation and I didn't get his phone number. He didn't own a cell phone and didn't care for them either. That's what he had told me, anyway.

Most likely the news of Nael's death reached him by way of his sheikh friends at the Swayleh mosque. They were associated with the mujahideen, according to what Nael had told me.

A man who must have been around fifty years old came to see me at the clothing store in Swayleh. All I knew about him was that his name was Sari and he was heavy set and fair skinned. He had thick hair parted on the right and a heavy mustache, which, like his hair, was black and speckled with silver-gray. And he spoke with confidence, though he was constantly looking all around himself.

He said he had come on behalf of Fawaz Basha.

"And who is Fawaz Basha?" I asked.

He said he had entrusted something into my custody.

"He has entrusted something into my custody and I don't know who he is?" I asked.

He looked me in the eye and said, "Mrs Umm al-Walid, I am talking about what Fawaz Basha entrusted to you on the trip to Paris, more than thirty years ago!"

I held back my astonishment and asked, "What did he entrust to me?"

He glanced over at the door to the store, then back at me. "The Basha's son. Where is he now?"

Then he proceeded to inform me that he knew all about what had transpired between Fawaz and me, and about my previous employment at the Malco Company, and the trip to Paris, and the son who was born seven months after my marriage. He told me it was in my best interest to answer his questions in order to keep my secret buried. Then he interjected a quick question, "I'm going to make things easy for you. Your son, Walid, where is he now?"

"I don't know," I replied.

He pursed his lips, opened his eyes wide and raised his eyebrows. "'The messenger's duty is but to convey the message.'[vi] I've given you my advice."

# Darrar al-Ghoury

I didn't know what secret lay behind the alarming task the man called Sari hired me to do after I got out of prison, where I'd been locked up in solitary confinement for seventy-five days and nights.

I didn't know where he got my address. How did that devil find me?

In this country, certain things went on that made a person feel vulnerable and as though his personal liberties had been violated and infringed upon. The paranoia was enough to drive a man insane.

Before this Sari character found me, I was baffled about how the Jordanian authorities were able to find out about our arrival from Afghanistan – myself and the three mujahideen who accompanied me – despite having shaved our beards and dressed in Western pants and shirts and suits.

Where did they get the information that led to our being arrested and charged with plotting terrorist activities in the country?

There were four of us – myself, a Moroccan mujahid brother, and two others from Iraq. We came all the way from Afghanistan and crossed into Jordan at the Iraqi border, but the security officers on the Jordanian side seized us before we could get our passports stamped. They were waiting for us, as I found out later on. They led us to an armored car and took off to a place that was unfamiliar to us at the time.

After getting us out of the car, they took each of us to a different location, and I never saw the three others again. They put me in solitary lock-up and tried to get information out of me about the mujahideen and their secrets.

As for why we came . . . we were given orders to go to Jordan and wait for some instructions and assistance we would receive once we arrived. That was all, no other directions or guidance.

They confronted us with lots of information I had thought was secret. Then they asked me if I preferred to be called by my original name, Shaher Abd al-Qadir Mahmoud al-Zarman, or by my jihadi name, Darrar al-Ghoury, and started laughing and jeering – may God's wrath fall upon them.

But I didn't know anything about the assignment we'd been sent to carry out, which it seemed was all part of the precautionary measures taken by the people who sent us.

A few days into their interrogation I could no longer sit down because of their abominable torture methods. Then I started spitting up blood and the soles of my feet turned the color of tar and what was left of my right ring finger also became infected – the one that was blown off by shrapnel from a bomb that exploded near me when I was in Afghanistan.

The cell was cramped and my chest also felt tight, to the point where one day I wished and prayed to God to forgive me for hurting myself and then proceeded to bang my forehead against the iron bars so hard that my forehead started to bleed. If it hadn't been for the prison guards who came to my aid and stitched up my forehead in one of their clinics, I might have lain there on the floor of my cell until I bled to death.

The remnants of that wound remained above my right eyebrow, in the form of a long scar, five centimeters in length.

In the prison cell there was nothing to read except a Holy Quran that had yellowed with age.

But even the Holy Quran was impossible to read in that loathsome cell that was like a grave above ground.

I felt claustrophobic again, like I was choking. The prison guards must have noticed my agitation and weakened state, and relayed that to their superiors, which was evident in the fact that they let up on interrogating me and hitting me in order to allow the panic attack to do the job. That was truly the severest punishment they could have imposed on me.

I came to the conclusion that torture was easier to bear than solitary confinement. At least when they were torturing me there was something happening and I could occupy myself with my pain as a way to feel time passing.

When I reached the breaking point again, I started screaming and pounding on the bars and the walls with my palms. Just a few days later they took me to the interrogation room. There the interrogator, who couldn't have been more than forty years old, informed me that they were going to keep me locked up in solitary indefinitely, and that he could help get me released on condition I divulged all the information and secrets I knew about the mujahideen brothers.

Then he stood up and said, "If you don't want to answer me now, I won't be able to see you again until a month from now and in the meantime you'll stay in solitary confinement."

I didn't answer. I started thinking, and he seemed to guess what was going through my mind because he picked up the phone and ordered me a cup of coffee.

I thought to myself: I know who I am, thank God. I fought in Afghanistan for eighteen months; I tended to numerous injuries; I asked to carry out a suicide bombing on a NATO camp but my captain didn't grant permission; with these two hands I have shot bullets at many an enemy and buried many a dutiful martyr as well.

But being placed in solitary confinement was much harsher than I could have imagined. My chest clamped up and I was short of breath. The world became tinier than the crack in a date pit. I began having wet dreams and soiling my clothes and had to remain in my impure state until it came time for my weekly bath. On the floor of that vile cell there was no point of reference. I could neither pray nor read the Holy Quran, which "none shall touch but those who are clean."[vii]

I couldn't tolerate being inside that cell, which tortured my soul, destroyed my convictions, and crushed my ability to be patient. I remembered that they knew a lot about me and the mujahideen, and I thought about what they wanted in return for my freedom. And I also recalled the words of the Sublime One in his precious book:

"On no soul doth Allah place a burden greater than it can bear. It gets every good that it earns, and it suffers every ill that it earns. (Pray:) 'Our Lord! Condemn us not if we forget or fall into error; our Lord! Lay not on us a burden Like that which Thou didst lay on those before us; Our Lord! Lay not on us a burden greater than we have strength to bear. Blot out our sins, and grant us forgiveness. Have mercy on us. Thou art our Protector; Help us against those who stand against faith.'"[viii]

The guard brought a cup of coffee and a glass of water, put them down in front of me, and left. I drank both quickly. The coffee was lukewarm.

I said to the interrogator, "Do you promise you will release me?"

He stood up from behind his desk and put down a stack of blank sheets of paper and a pen. Then he said to me, "I knew you would use your head. Now you will go to your cell and write down everything you know. If what you write is truthful and contains information of use to us, then we will let you go in a matter of days. And remember that we can tell the difference between fabrications and the truth." He smiled as he said this. Then he turned to leave and added, "Tomorrow I will come for you at this same time to see what you have written."

He called for the guard to escort me back to my cell with the pen and paper.

## Samah Shahadeh

I never liked politics, and I got fed up with what they labeled the "Arab Spring."

My father, too, was quite agitated by what was happening.

I liked the description he gave to Fawaz one evening. "In every person's heart," he said, "there is a secret and an innate being. What's happening in our Arab world is that this being has broken free of his chains and burst onto the world ready to kill and smash and destroy whatever is in its path, with the savage brutality of a Hollywood horror movie."

And when Fawaz asked him if this being was ever going to stop, he said, "Absolutely not. There is nothing indicating it is possible for him to return to his hiding place. At least not in the foreseeable future."

As far as Fawaz was concerned, all that mattered was the effect the situation was having on his interests in Arab countries and in Jordan, where one couldn't be sure how long we would stay out of the fire.

For me, it wasn't so much about the effect on interests as it was about all the killing and the blood and the repression, and also my desire for life to remain stable in our world.

Fawaz told me that Uroub told Sari that the people of Syria would be in conflict for ten years, and would be divided into four nations, and afterwards they would spend ten years rebuilding their country.

"And what about Jordan?" I asked him. "Why didn't you ask her that, Fawaz?"

Sarcastically, he answered, "Someone hearing you might think Uroub's sayings are divine revelations. What's your problem, Samah?"

He was right. I had been too quick with my question. It sounded like I was sure everything Uroub said was really going to happen.

Fawaz tried to catch me up from time to time, to make himself look smarter than me.

I felt as though he laid snares for me, so I might get caught trying to escape the net of my patience – my distinguishing characteristic. Actually, that didn't bother me so much. His traps were clever and not too harsh.

I thought about what he had told me Uroub said with regards to dying at the hands of a thirty-year-old man. Could that have been one of his traps?

When I visited my father at his house after a three-week absence, he scrutinized my face and looked me up and down. I felt – as I always did – like a little child in his presence despite my fifty-seven years. He was the only thing I had left connecting me to my childhood and my youth.

"What's bothering you, Samah?" he asked.

"Nothing," I answered. "I just missed you."

He threw his head back in a manner that made me think he didn't believe me. "Your face is emaciated, and so is the rest of you."

I looked down at my chest and my legs. I remembered how the waistband of the black trousers I put on before leaving the house had felt a little loose, and how I also had to brighten up my cheeks with some make-up so they wouldn't look so gaunt. I had chalked it up to the effects of time. Before I snapped out of my daydream, my father ordered the housekeeper to bring the bathroom scale. Then he asked, "When was the last time you weighed yourself?"

"Fawaz's birthday," I answered.

"How much did you weigh then?"

"Around sixty-five kilos," I said in a manner indicating I wasn't sure.

The housekeeper came back carrying the scale. She placed it on the carpet and I stood on it. How great was my shock when I saw the needle pointing to the number fifty-five.

He peered into my face again and said, "You can prevent me from knowing what's going on with you, but you can't hide that you're emaciated!"

"It's nothing, Father," I said in a fluster. "Nothing. Would I dare hide something from you?"

He appeared unconvinced. I felt he had discovered my lie, but then he shook his head and said, "I was going to say to you that you're free like fathers say to their children in order to place the responsibility for their actions on them, but you're not like that."

Forgetting I was a grown-up, I childishly protested, "What do mean, Father?"

"What is worrying you?" he asked without looking me in the face.

# Darrar al-Ghoury

When I had reached the age of twenty-six, I knew for certain that I'd chosen a thorny path in life that was full of land mines, but I'd always believed it was the only path.

Now I was starting to see that there were many other roads to take in this life. Roads with fewer thorns and land mines and possibly more benefits.

The interrogator was true to his word. They let me go two days after I gave my statement. But when I complained that life had turned its back on me, he said, "It's not life that has turned its back on you. You are the one sitting backwards."

How did he come up with this expression I had heard once before?

I returned to my father's house, hoping to share with my parents and my siblings the burden of making a living in Mashari', our village in the Jordan Valley, and to start a new life.

I had a feeling of nostalgia for the market place and its shops, so I decided to go take a stroll. I noticed that people who knew me pretended not to know me, or moved out of my path, or at best shook my hand quickly and made excuses about having to tend to some matter.

I borrowed a motorcycle from one of my relatives and took a drive through the Valley's fields and villages. I thought about this world and what I had come to be – a young man with a Bachelor's degree in nursing he didn't know what to do with. The country was full of nurses, male and female, and even if I did find a job, surely the security forces would bar me from joining any clinic or medical center.

What was I to do, without a single dinar in my pocket, while people chased desperately after life and withdrew into themselves and to their money, snubbed each other and plotted against each other? My father worked as a low-level municipal employee, barely making enough to feed my three brothers and my mother.

But, praise be to God, less than a month after getting out of prison, this man called Sari contacted me and told me that he had a job opportunity for me and wanted to see me.

I said to myself that maybe relief from my misery had been sent to me from Almighty God.

I went to Amman and waited for him on a street called Rainbow Street in Jabal Amman, in some café with a strange foreign name.

He was the one who chose the place when he contacted me. He had said, "Just tell the taxi driver 'Rainbow Street' and he will take you there."

I hadn't been waiting more than a few minutes when a fifty-year-old man came through the café entrance. He had a white face and a black mustache with touches of gray.

He was wearing an ash-gray suit with a white shirt and no necktie. He came directly to the table where I was sitting, as if he knew me.

I said to myself: Please God grant me an easy path and loosen my tongue for me.

I stood up. "Hello, Shaher," he said, shaking my hand. "I'm Sari."

I greeted him and introduced myself, noting that he did not give me his full name.

He looked me over from head to toe. I was wearing a yellow shirt and black trousers. I felt embarrassed by my old shoes which, on top of being dusty and faded, were too tight on my feet.

I sought refuge in God and asked for His aid. Then I summoned up my strength after Sari sat down across the table from me and I said, "I am very happy to know you have work for me. May God compensate you for your good deed. But please permit me to ask a question. Where did you get my phone number?"

"Let's agree on something," he said with an air of superiority. "From now on, no questions outside the parameters of the job I am going to ask you to do. And before we get started, let me tell you that I know you were with the mujahideen in Afghanistan, and that the name they gave you was Darrar al-Ghoury. I will call you by that name from now on instead of Shaher. I also know everything that happened to you, and if you ask me, 'Where did you get this information?' I will tell you that is my business. I have an entire center for research and information and I can get any information I want about you or anyone else for that matter, so don't bother asking."

"Did you find out why they released me?" I asked.

"I told you," he answered. "No questions unless they have something to do with the job I want you to do. And now let me explain the mission I have for you."

I was puzzled. Where did he get such authoritativeness? It filled his words with a level of sincerity and fortitude that sent terror right into the soul. But my bewilderment disappeared once I found out what it was he wanted from me.

He asked me to return to the ranks of the mujahideen in Afghanistan, and to find a mujahid by the name of Walid Nael Shaker Dughaybil, whose jihadi name was Sharhabil.

He spoke as if he possessed the same level of authority as the people who had tortured and imprisoned me, maybe more.

Before I could say anything, he reached into his pocket and said, "I believe you need money now, because you aren't working."

"I'll be fine, God willing," I said proudly.

He handed me a white envelope and said, "Five hundred dinars. It will help you make your decision. Then we will agree on the rest."

I asked myself whether this was a blessing coming to me out of the blue from God, or was it a trap they wanted me to fall into all over again? Who knew who this Sari fellow was? And who sent him? And why did he choose me in particular?

While I was thinking through all this, he got up, looking at his watch, and said, "We will meet again in two days. I will call you."

Then he handed me a little slip of white paper with a cell phone number and no other information written on it.

"This is my number in case it gets erased from your phone," he said and then left. I stayed behind, thinking.

But I didn't stay long. I remembered that I had 500 dinars in my hands, which was a substantial sum of money to me in those difficult circumstances. I was afraid something unexpected might happen, so I got up and left.

I headed immediately downtown, bought a pair of comfortable shoes and put them on. I stuck my old pair in a bag and tossed it into the first trash can I came across. Then I sauntered over to Hashem's Restaurant, ate two plates of *hummus* and *foule*[ix] and more than twenty pieces of falafel, thanking God for his generosity.

On the bus that took me from Amman back to my village I started thinking. If the down payment was 500 dinars, how much would I get for carrying out the mission? Five hundred dinars just like that, no receipt, no nothing.

I said to myself: Let this be the beginning of a new adventure in life, as long as there is money in return. And anyway, after I did what he asked, I could repent. I could go and perform the Umrah pilgrimage or the Hajj, and from there I could turn to God in sincere repentance, for God is forgiving and merciful, but after I pocketed enough money to open a little business of some sort, maybe even a little grocery shop. I could give alms to the poor and show mercy if God presented me with the opportunity. The important thing now was to find Walid . . . or Sharhabil.

The first thing my mother noticed when I got home was my shiny new shoes. Her eyes were drawn to them the moment I walked through the door. She asked me if I had found some work, so I answered her, "Put your faith in God. Soon I will be working."

Two days later I met up with Sari in the same location. I told him I accepted the mission and also made it clear that it was going to require some time. He acknowledged with a nod of his head. And when I told him that I had signed an affidavit with the Intelligence Office attesting that I would not return to the mujahideen, he said, "Forget the affidavit. Consider yourself released from it."

"Suppose they prevent me from leaving the country?" I said. "This is very likely."

"We will deal with things as they come up. Every problem has a solution," he said. "Just get yourself ready as soon as possible."

Then he asked to see my cell phone, so I showed it to him. It was a cheap one.

"Perfect," he said. "You don't want to appear to have a lot of money over there."

Then he gave me a more advanced model and showed me how to use it. He made it clear that I shouldn't let the mujahideen see me with it and I should only let them see the old cheap one. That was if they even allowed me to use it.

## Abu Hudhayfah

I marveled at Sharhabil's skill during the first battle he engaged in as a member of our base. I had never seen anything like it. By God he destroyed machinery like a professional hunter shooting down prey, turning it into black scum the way lightning turns Afghan spider trees into charred, black sticks. He hunkered down behind a boulder shaded by a tree, around 200 meters from our position. There he was able to take cover from the gunfire that was being fired from their tanks and was coming close to us. Then he fired his first rocket, destroying one of their tanks, which went up in smoke. It gave us a target to fire at with our machine guns from numerous positions, making us seem like an entire battalion of mujahideen. Then one of our mujahideen brothers by the name of Anas al-Yamani came out of his trench carrying two hand grenades and headed towards the second tank, screaming. But he was martyred before he could throw them, may God have mercy on his soul and let him enter His spacious Paradise.

When Sharhabil destroyed a second tank, we were exuberant, because this gave us a boost and helped us to transition from a defensive position to an offensive one. The rest of the tanks turned around in retreat.

God is with you, Sharhabil! How sharp is your aim. It reminds one of the arrows shot by the Prophet's Companions during the great Battle of Badr. And how admirable is your modesty and lack of need to brag about your deeds.

After the armored vehicles withdrew, we inspected the battlefield to discover that six of the mujahideen had been martyred, including Anas al-Yamani.

We gave them a hasty burial so that we could vacate our hideout temporarily, in case they came back with reinforcements.

However – Glory be to You, O God! – I swear the fragrance of musk rose up from the corpses of our martyrs and the area around them with the dawn of that misty morning. And when we buried them, that delightful smell continued to waft its way into my nostrils, filling me with a strong desire to win that martyrdom which God – most precious and most glorious – had not willed to bestow upon me during that great battle.

As for the miracle I bore witness to in the vicinity of that hideout, it occurred forty days later. When we returned to that place to straighten the martyrs' bodies and direct them towards the *kiblah*, the smell of musk emanated from their graves when we opened them, and we found them still clothed and soaked in their blood, just as we had buried them, without change. We cried, "*Allahu akbar*" and "*La ilaha illa llah*" and embraced each other exuberantly.

I praise you, O God, for the grace of jihad and for your miracles, which you have showered upon the mujahideen, your good and righteous servants.

# Muntaha al-Rayyeh

The worst thing about Sari's visit was the way he treated me, as if he was coming to bring charges against me or had some kind of evidence on me. He acted like someone who knew I had committed the sin of adultery, and who I had committed it with.

Why did I say, "Like someone who knew"? The fact of the matter was that he would not have come to me unless he did know. Maybe in his mind I was a whore, or some other word.

I sensed in the tone of his voice and the things he said to me a kind of threat, as well as the stirring up of a past I had buried long, long ago.

"What secret are you referring to?" I said, trying to tone down his threat. "What secret are you going to spill? To who? My husband, who's been dead for more than four years?"

"'He who uses his head will not grow weary,'" he said.

It was clear he wasn't going to leave without getting something out of me, some kind of information about al-Walid at the very least.

"Al-Walid is with the mujahideen in Afghanistan," I said. "What do you want with him?"

"It's not me," he said. "It's his father, the Basha, who wants to see him. It's his right. Is he still in Afghanistan?"

"He hasn't come here since he left," I said crossly. "Ask at the borders. Ask at the airport."

Calmly, but with determination, he said, "I know that he has not returned via the borders or the airports. But I heard he entered the country secretly, in which case there is no doubt he would come visit his mother."

I felt he was not being truthful with what he said. Maybe he was trying to play with my mind, though I hadn't said anything other than the truth.

I looked directly into his eyes and said, "You haven't told me, what does your boss Fawaz want from him exactly?"

He averted his eyes. "Mrs Muntaha, or Umm al-Walid, the Basha wants his son, and you yourself know, 'No debt goes unpaid if the collector comes calling.'"

My sense of irritation came back. "You talk as if he were a little boy in diapers."

He put a business card on the table with his name and phone number. "In any case," he said, "my phone number is on this card if you decide to use your head."

I remembered Fawaz's insult after the trip to Paris. I got a hold of myself and said in a nasty tone, "Listen. Tell your boss Fawaz al-Shardah that al-Walid is a thirty-year-old man now who has taken up killing people in Afghanistan. He has killed many. Who knows, he could come back here at any moment and I would tell him to go back. If I were in Fawaz's shoes or your shoes, I would be careful."

## Sari Abu Amineh

How mind boggling. Mrs Muntaha said that her son Walid, or al-Walid as she calls him, might come here. Then she warned me to watch out for him. And her warning was directed at me and the Basha.

She actually threatened us with her son.

I went to her to deliver a strong message from the Basha, and she ended up giving me a stronger one to deliver to him.

Could Uroub's prophecy come true at the hands of this sixty-year-old woman, Muntaha al-Rayyeh, who I'd searched for for such a long time?

What was there to stop her from seeking her son's help? Most likely she called him from time to time. I was almost certain she was in contact with him in some way or another. She was his mother after all, and he was her son, and a mother cannot be completely cut off from her son for ten years or more.

She could turn him against us and he could come to hurt us, or even kill us. It made no difference to people like that. He had nothing to fear.

If his mother were to turn him against us, I would expect him to become incensed.

Of course the matter wasn't as simple as that. His demise could come at our hands, but everything was possible. He could come after us even before finding out that his mother had been an adulteress before she got married and that the Basha was his real father.

Women are the source of so many problems.

All she had to do was tell him a non-believer was threatening her in her own home or in her shop.

I noticed that Mrs Muntaha was not fat or flabby like most women her age, and her fair-complexioned face still retained some of its beauty despite her being nearly sixty years old. Even her bangs, which stuck out a little from beneath her white scarf, were black and showed no signs of gray.

Actually, her face reminded me of the actress Shams al-Baroudy. I wondered if she looked like her when she was young.

# Darrar al-Ghoury

I went to Al-Shouneh al-Shamaliyah, to the home of Sheikh Abd al-Karim al-Abbas, the one who enlisted me twenty-two months earlier and sent me to carry out jihad in Afghanistan.

He welcomed me warmly – may God reward him for that – as though he were reuniting with a son after a long absence. Then he sat me down beside him there in his room on a mattress up against the wall whose paint was peeling off. He started asking what had happened to me.

I thanked God that he wasn't aware of what had happened to me in prison. That was clear from the conversation, for he commended me for my resolve and for getting out with my head held high, as he put it.

I asked him about the three mujahideen who accompanied me on the homeward journey to Jordan and he answered that he had no knowledge of their whereabouts or of what had happened to them.

I spoke to him about the blessings of jihad and self-sacrifice for the sake of God, and about the mujahideen vying with each other to achieve martyrdom, and I broke down into tears.

He patted me on the shoulder with his right hand, in which he held a long set of prayer beads, and said, "Are you so moved by this that you would cry, Darrar?"

"Yes, sir," I said. "They deprived me of the blessing of jihad and martyrdom when they arrested me and put me in their prison cell."

"God is with you, my son," he said. "He who wages holy war for the sake of God but is unable to achieve the blessing of jihad, or martyrdom, despite his efforts, will still be considered a martyr if he dies a contrite Muslim seeking God's forgiveness."

My voice softened to the point of sounding feeble and submissive. "Sheikh, sir, jihad is my only means of rescue and escape from the estrangement I have been living since getting out of prison – estrangement from my parents, brothers, friends, neighbors, and acquaintances. They all look at me with disdain, and shun me. They avoid me like an infectious disease and call me a terrorist, even though jihad for the sake of God is not considered terrorism except by non-believers and apostates. They say I've ruined my future, forgetting that there is no future in this world or in the hereafter except in Paradise. And they blame me for lack of work, forgetting that the best work is to worship the one true God, and to carry out religious duty and jihad for His sake. That is how they have treated me since I came back, so please let me return, sir, into the folds of jihad, into the ranks of the mujahideen who are as pure and clear as ice and snow."

He nodded his head and said, "Why such astonishment, Darrar? Islam began as a stranger and will go back to being a stranger. 'Blessed are the strangers.' That is what our Noble Prophet – prayers and the peace of God be upon him – said, more than 1,400 years ago."

"I am but a stranger who cannot live amongst these unbelievers," I said. "So free me into jihad. Free me so I can win martyrdom and see with my own eyes the *houris* of Paradise, for they pluck the strings in the presence of the prophets and the righteous and the martyrs."

"Will they permit you to cross the borders?" he asked.

"I will find a way to smuggle myself out," I answered. "Sir, he who has tasted jihad cannot but return to it again."

"And what if they catch you, Darrar?" he asked.

"I am accustomed to their prisons," I said. "There is no difference to me between that small prison and this grand prison. I want to carry out what my religion demands of me, so I will not feel regret every time I hear about an attack carried out by my mujahideen brothers without me. Sir, I've become like a fish. I can only live in the sea of jihad and the mujahideen."

"Put your trust in God. I will do what I can," he said. "Ask God to grant success and good fortune."

I wasn't faking my tears in front of him, and I wasn't truthful either. It was a mixture of truth and falsehood, and I felt I had lost my conviction. But I was intent on going back to Afghanistan with the blessing and confirmation of Sheikh al-Abbas, who I felt sympathized with me and wished for me to return.

## Sari Abu Amineh

The Basha was never a coward.

Once, three years earlier, the airplane we were in on our way to Madrid hit some turbulence and dropped more than 200 feet to a hard landing, causing the contents of the overhead bins to come crashing down on us. The Basha kept calm and held his composure. He was the only passenger who didn't show signs of fright or start screaming and trembling and reciting the Quran, or making the sign of the cross over their chests.

I, on the other hand, shuddered with fear and recited the *shahada* for my life in a trembling voice.

During the Davos conference he participated in in Switzerland a few years back, he didn't heed the advice of the conference organizers to wait a while before leaving the auditorium in order to avoid the protestors – men and women with their chests bared – who were demonstrating outside.

He was not a coward, not to my knowledge. However, one recent morning, he called on his driver and his security guard to stop a bearded man he had seen driving down the street in front of his house in a rundown Opal. He had noticed the man while standing on the balcony that overlooks the *houri* fountain in his garden. He drove past once and then came back again and again, and from what I understood he was driving very slowly and was peeking inside the gate in a suspicious manner.

The guard and the driver stopped him and made him get out of the car. They could see he was wearing a short *dishdasha* robe, the kind fundamentalists wear. They searched his car and didn't find anything suspicious. The guard asked him why he kept driving back and forth down a road that only people who knew the neighborhood used, which was only a few people. He said he was looking for the house of someone who was expecting him, and he gave the man's name. When the guard recognized the name, he explained how to find the house and followed him in his car to make sure he arrived at the big house nearby that was owned by a well-known food industry merchant. He waited to make sure the owner of the house actually received the bearded man into his house.

When the Basha told me about the incident, he wasn't angry or frightened. Rather he told me the story with an air of lightheartedness and with pity for the man.

But I understood what that air of lightheartedness was hiding in terms of questions directed to me. And so I contacted that wretch named Shaher al-Zarman, or Darrar al-Ghoury, to make sure he was getting prepared for travel and was committed to carrying out the mission I had hired him to do.

I forgave the Basha for treating that man that way, for I recalled the warning Mrs Muntaha al-Rayyeh gave me when I met with her, and which I hadn't relayed to the Basha.

## Darrar al-Ghoury

That Sari fellow was a blue *jinn*, God damn him. The type who wouldn't let anything stop him from getting what he wanted.

He managed to arrange my exit via the Jordanian-Iraqi border, in a pick-up driven by a silent man wearing black glasses that covered nearly half his face. He dropped me off in the city of Ar Rutba and got back in his car without my seeing his face or knowing who he was.

I got to Baghdad and headed to a café on Al-Rashid Street. It was a blistering hot day and the smell of tobacco mingled with the smell of grilled meat and the foul odor of raw chicken from the neighboring shops.

I looked around at the people sitting on the wooden chairs and noticed a man sitting behind a round worktable. He had a brown file placed in front of him and a set of brown prayer beads in his right hand. He was fanning his face with a piece of yellow cardboard.

He's the one I'm looking for, I said to myself. He fit the description Sheikh Al-Abbas gave me when he sent me.

Then I pulled my set of brown prayer beads with the yellow thread out from my pocket and started fiddling with the beads with both hands as I approached him, saying, "'God suffices me, and He is the best Guardian.'"

He looked at my prayer beads and then at my face. He signaled with his eyes for me to sit down next to him.

He poured me some black tea and then escorted me to a house below street level near Zawra Park, where I stayed for two nights. Then I took a plane to Pakistan. I was greeted in the Hyderabad Airport by two young Pakistani brothers who were waiting inside the gate area. One of them carried out the tasks of stamping the passport and other entry requirements with surprising ease and speed. He moved about the airport as if it was his own house. Then he escorted me and his friend to a house in the basement of a mosque where I spent the night.

The next morning they sent me to Kandahar in a truck transporting provisions and medical supplies. I got out near a warehouse associated with the city hospital they called the Shafa Khana. Then the driver turned me over to an Afghan man who took me to a mujahideen hideout I'd never seen before.

## Samah Shahadeh

I was in the habit of strolling through the garden every morning, to breathe in the fresh air and inspect the trees and the bird cages and the flower beds.

From time to time I would water them with the sprayer attached to the hose.

I found that kind of work gratifying.

After the incident with the bearded man who was driving his car outside our house, I started to feel fearful.

The peace of mind that had permeated our home ever since we built it two decades earlier started to wither away from my life.

The security measures I started noticing didn't come from nowhere.

Fawaz himself had grown more cautious than before. He perked his ears whenever he heard the sound of a car engine approaching our house. Sometimes he would call the guard or the driver, and speak with him in his office. Even his posture when standing out on the balcony lacked the usual confidence.

His eye gestures and body movements started showing signs of something unusual going on.

"This isn't fair," I said to him. "You have to tell me what's going on."

He answered me with little patience, "I already told you. Have you forgotten?"

"Told me what, Fawaz?" I asked.

"What the fortune-teller Uroub said. Have you forgotten?"

"So this means you believe what she told you about a thirty-year-old man wanting to kill you?"

"I don't believe it, but caution is warranted."

I let out a sigh. "If this type of caution is warranted, then I should take precautions as well."

"Precautions against what?"

"The cat that came back to life."

"What cat, Samah?"

"Uroub interpreted a dream I had the night before your birthday. I saw a cat coming out of the wall. It shook the dust off its head and came back to life. Uroub told me I was going to discover a secret that had been kept from me. Are you hiding something from me, Fawaz?"

He was silent at first and then said, "After we got married – if you remember – I suggested that you get a house cat, and you refused because you could not live in the same place with a cat. When it became clear to me and to you that we would not be able to have children, I suggested getting a cat again, but you refused. And the night of my sixtieth birthday, I noticed that the wife of one of my friends brought her cat with her, so I asked myself once again, 'Why does Samah hate cats so much? Why don't I revive the idea of getting a pet cat?'"

When he finished that last sentence, he peered into my face with eyes open wide beneath a pair of raised eyebrows. "That is the meaning of the dream you had in your sleep," he said.

Then he stood up and said, "I think I am entitled to revive my old wish of having a cat in my house."

I immediately said, "In that case, you and your cat can go live somewhere else, anywhere but here in this house."

This made him burst out in laughter.

What did he find so funny?

# Abu Hudhayfah

Sharhabil was very quiet, a man of action who stayed out of the fray. I felt this calmness of his contained a storehouse of formidable jihadi powers.

That was not all, either. He was also an avid reader of books on Shari'a, in addition to the Holy Quran, whenever he got the chance.

Indeed God guided Sharhabil's steps and enabled him to fire his rockets right into the hearts of the unbelievers, right through their armor, on numerous occasions. He fought ferociously in more than twenty-three battles, and rescued seven wounded mujahideen before they could be taken prisoner. In one of the battles he was hit in his right thigh by shrapnel and was treated by an Afghan doctor who operated on him without giving him anesthesia or anything to numb him.

I suppose with that Sharhabil paid the price of the *houri* that would be waiting for him in eternal Paradise.

But there was one matter about Sharhabil I was not able to understand or to ask him about, which was that he never talked about his family like the rest of us. I felt that this aspect of his life was not open to discussion or deliberation. If he hadn't been required to write the name of his mother in the mujahideen registration form our commander entrusted me with, I never would have found out that the name of this great mother was Muntaha Rasim Salah al-Rayyeh.

When we carried out a reconnaissance mission near the NATO base in Kandahar, Sharhabil asked our commander, Abu al-Zubayr, for permission to carry out a suicide attack at the checkpoint leading to that base which was impeding our progress and causing many martyrs to be felled from our ranks, but Abu al-Zubayr refused.

"Say God is one, Sharhabil," he said to him. "We are in desperate need of your rocket launching ability, Sharhabil, not your body."

And when the fighting intensified between us and the war machines and soldiers at that checkpoint, a number of mujahideen were wounded, among them Sharhabil, who took a dastardly bullet to the lower part of his shoulder. The next day we asked for aid and reinforcements, so they sent us medical supplies and a Jordanian mujahid medic called Darrar al-Ghoury. He was olive-complexioned and slim and had a very noticeable large scar on his forehead. He had a yellow tint to his eyes as though from a liver infection.

He came up from the southern hideout to Kandahar to treat our eleven wounded mujahideen.

Darrar treated Sharhabil, and extracted the bullet from below his shoulder. Then he moved on to the other wounded men and treated them as best he could, using medical supplies he brought with him.

After he finished taking care of the rest of the mujahideen, he remained vigilant over Sharhabil, who kept falling in and out of consciousness. I felt as though that mujahid had come to us by the grace of God, the Most High, the All-Powerful, in order to bring Sharhabil back to life.

But then after a while I started feeling that Darrar al-Ghoury was going too far with his care for Sharhabil, insisting on staying with him in the medical care trench. I also noticed that he was overly cautious and suspicious of everything. When I asked him about it he answered that his experience getting arrested at the Jordanian borders taught him not to give his trust so easily and to be skeptical before putting faith in people. Then he asked me, "Abu Hudhayfah, how do you explain the Jordanian security forces knowing all about our arrival and arresting us before we could get our passports stamped at the borders?"

I asked for God's forgiveness and cursed the spies and traitors in all times and all places. And I recited the holy verse from *Surat al-Anfal* (The Spoils of War):

"O ye that believe! betray not the trust of Allah and the Messenger, nor misappropriate knowingly things entrusted to you."[x]

# Darrar al-Ghoury

God eased the way for me, and right away I was able to locate Walid, who was known by the name Sharhabil. I was called to his hideout to treat the wounded there, because the doctor in that area was busy treating the wounded in other places. I tended to Sharhabil's wound and removed a bullet from him the size of a thumb.

He was in and out of consciousness. His face and long hair and beard were all soaked with sweat, as though he had a high fever, and I could see his lips reciting the *shahada* whenever he came to.

I took several pictures of him with the cell phone I got from Sari.

After taking the pictures, I went outside the treatment room made from adobe and sat on a nearby rock.

It was pitch dark outside and I didn't know what happened to me. I had thought I would send the photos I took of Sharhabil to Sari. But how could I do that to a mujahid who had been entrusted to me? How could I stand before my God on Judgment Day with the face of a traitor?

I said to myself: Sari is not to be taken lightly. He told me it was within his power to send information to the mujahideen informing them I was collaborating with suspicious entities if I didn't stick to our agreement.

He said that it was also within his power to supply them – by way of his connections – with proof, and that was what made me lose my mind. Where did he get proof?

Then I suddenly wondered: Could he have been recording my voice during our meetings?

By God, I didn't rule anything out when it came to that wretch Sari, despite all the money he gave me, a portion of which I gave to my brothers and parents before leaving Jordan. When they asked me about it I told them that is was an allowance from the mujahideen to cover my travel and other expenses.

An ordeal, by God it was an ordeal and a horrible trial.

A Saudi mujahid brother called Abu Hudhayfah approached me. He was around thirty-three years old, olive complexion, shaved head, black beard, and shaved mustache. His two front teeth had a space between them that cut his smile in half. He asked me what was wrong and I said, "I'm sad for Sharhabil, actually. He wakes from unconsciousness to say the *shahada* and then slips back under."

"And what do you think of his wound?" he asked.

"He will live, God willing," I said. "But he will need two to three weeks."

After Sharhabil got better I returned to my camp in south Kandahar, treating the wounded and assisting the doctor with his surgeries. I would withdraw into myself from time to time, thinking and reflecting about what I had gotten myself into.

I no longer had any doubt that Sari wanted to get rid of Sharhabil because he posed a huge danger to the Americans in Afghanistan and that Sari was connected with the intelligence apparatus. That apparatus was bent on doing something to help the NATO forces in concerted effort with the CIA, who it seemed had sought their help to get rid of Sharhabil.

Otherwise, what could explain Sari's excessive concern for Sharhabil? Why did he want to get rid of him? What did he stand to gain?

## Sari Abu Amineh

Anxiety had taken hold of the Basha.

He was intent on preempting events by getting rid of his illegitimate son before the reverse could happen. He started asking me from time to time if my plan had worked and how it was progressing. I would tell him everything was fine, and when I said to him, "But the plan is going to be costly," he answered in a tone not lacking in expertise, "Does a fishing rod catch a fish without some bait attached?"

Whenever the Basha clasped his hands behind his back and started pacing back and forth it became difficult to look him in the eye while listening to him.

He told me once that pacing gave rise to new ideas and facilitated conversation. I had no choice but to agree with what he said. He stopped pacing and faced me, saying, "Are you just trying to humor me, Sari?"

"Actually," I said, "you've made me aware of something new, and I like it."

It was true that the Basha had changed since hearing from Uroub and Harsha al-Hakim. He now did a lot more listening than he did talking. Sometimes he would take refuge in his office. He would tend to the plants in there and listen to flute music. But at times he seemed nervous, which was also unusual for him.

One time I said to him, "Will you be able to live with the notion that a young man, who is your own flesh and blood, will die?"

"My own flesh and blood?" he said mockingly. "What does that mean? I live my life without such silly notions. Anyone who wants to destroy me must die before he can execute his plan, even if the chances of it happening are only one in a thousand. The important thing is that the chance is out there."

"As you wish, Basha," I said. "Walid will die before he can touch a single hair on your head."

Then he added, as if there was something he had forgotten, "This whole question of fathers and sons is nothing but the splitting of a cell. Each new cell becomes a world of its own, unconnected to the other except by heredity. It's possible for one to attack the other and finish it off."

I remembered my son, Suhayl, and my daughter, Suhayla, both of whom I would not trade for all the treasures in the world and for whom I would sacrifice my very soul. Then I asked myself whether it was possible for a father to kill his own flesh and blood even if the son was illegitimate. Was it possible for people to think of their progeny as the mere division of cells like the Basha talked about?

I shook my head and asked him again, "If Walid is indeed killed, what will we do with Darrar?"

"We will see when the time comes," he said.

That was what made me recall the image of that desperate fellow, Darrar al-Ghoury, the one who could rescue the Basha from his fate. Or, rather, the one who could force fate to change its course.

## Muntaha al-Rayyeh

I hadn't really planned on saying what I said to Sari when he came to see me; it just came out spontaneously, in response to his arrogance.

But after he left, those words transformed into an idea worthy of consideration. If Fawaz al-Shardah was sending someone to ask me about al-Walid and to warn me, then that meant he had bad intentions towards me or al-Walid.

It was possible Sari interpreted what I said as a threat to him and his boss.

I hoped that was the case, for I feared no one in this world. I spent my old age alone in my house with no husband or son or daughter to occupy me in my loneliness, or care for me if something were to happen to me. I would sit for hours in front of the television, stricken with boredom. I busied myself with sweeping and mopping the floor twice a day despite my aching back. I cooked enough food to feed a whole family and shared it with the neighbors sometimes. I bathed and changed my clothes every day, and looked in the mirror at my face, which had changed a lot. I observed the lower parts of my cheeks as they sagged below the corners of my mouth. I looked at my neck and saw the effects time was having on it. Occasionally my mother came to visit and stayed over a night or two, but she quickly grew bored and went back home, leaving me all alone once again. My father didn't visit anymore; he was debilitated by diabetes and could hardly see.

Sometimes I wished the sun would hurry up and rise so I could go to the shop. There was some semblance of life there at least. I interacted with people and there were people all around, talking and working. There were cars and bicycles and vendor carts out on the street, and people. I even started opening the shop at seven every morning, long before the owners of the nearby shops up and down the long avenue even woke up, except for the baker who didn't close his doors all night long.

After Sari's visit, I remembered Fawaz and that sinful trip to Paris with all its details.

Why shouldn't Fawaz pay for abusing me? Why should I leave that wound open if I had the opportunity to avenge myself?

By sending Sari to see me and ask me all those direct and personal questions, Fawaz had awakened all that had been lodged inside me for such a long time, wiping the dust off of what all those years had buried.

## Abu Hudhayfah

After Sharhabil recovered, thank God, and was able once again to hold the rocket launcher on his shoulder, there were new developments.

The regime in Damascus grew bloodthirsty for Sunni Muslims, killing tens of thousands of them. By God, of all the violent plots and schemes concocted by the enemies of Islam, this was the most violent and posed the greatest danger to the *Ummah* of Muhammad. That was what our commander said when he sent Sharhabil, me, and five others on a secret mission to Syria to explore the situation there before opening the door to jihad in that afflicted Islamic country.

Bits of news came to us one after another, causing the blood to boil in our veins, especially when we learned that legions of Nusairis and Rafidites had united with the lands of Persia, Iraq, Lebanon, and Yemen to fight against the Sunnis and Al-Gama'a.[xi] I swear that was one of the decisive wars dividing the camp of right from the camp of wrong.

We went to Syria by way of Turkey, through a tunnel near the town of Jarabulus. There we were met by some Arab mujahideen who gave us heavy clothing to wear the moment we arrived and then sent us in a truck to a camp belonging to the Deir al-Zor region.

The camp was vast and extended across two hills, each with a water cistern at the summit, and lowlands where the six jihadi groups trained. They trained whenever they had the opportunity. Each group had a commander who reported directly to the commander of the entire camp – Commander Al-Thuqafy with the hollow cheeks, bony face and mustache draping over the sides of his mouth. They put us together with the Suqoor al-Duru' group, the Hawks of Armor, because of what they knew of Sharhabil, the "slayer of armor."

But the situation in Syria differed a great deal from the situation in Afghanistan. The houses were all demolished, the streets were all torn up, and the distance between warring fighters was short. The mujahideen would attack and withdraw, kill and be martyred in huge numbers, and the supplies and food were plentiful.

## Sari Abu Amineh

I called Darrar, because he still hadn't done anything, despite all the gifts I showered on him and his family – things they never dreamed of acquiring. The Basha continued to ask me what was happening with Walid and I kept telling him everything was going according to plan.

"Good to know you're still alive," I said to Darrar. "You can thank me for that. But I can't wait forever. I think you know what I mean."

Darrar said some things that shocked me. From what I understood, Walid had left Afghanistan, and Darrar wasn't able to find out where he was headed to because of the covert nature of the mission he had been sent to carry out, but he was still trying to reach him.

I asked him angrily what he had been doing when Sharhabil disappeared, and why he was so calm about having lost track of him. He kept repeating the same thing, "Mr Sari, I am still trying to reach him."

Here began the real danger; Walid had disappeared and might have come to Jordan to carry out some sort of mission.

That terrifying notion rambled through my mind and heart. I remembered what Uroub said about the Basha's demise coming at the hands of his son, and I started leaning in favor of believing that Walid had surely come to Jordan to carry out a mission that would result in the Basha's death, despite the absurdity of it all and reliance on fortune-tellers' prophesies.

I thought it over and came to the conclusion that I must tell the Basha. Who knew? My guess might turn out to be true, and every precaution had to be taken.

Then I remembered Mrs Muntaha's warning and threats that day when I went to see her. I felt the circle had narrowed, leaving only one possibility – the time had come. And so I met privately with the Basha in his office and shared with him all the information I had, including the fact that Walid had left Afghanistan and all about Mrs Muntaha's threats to me and to him.

Then I suggested seeking help from the brilliant Grand Basha, Nayef Shahadeh. With eyes widened and eyebrows raised the Basha said to me, "Why are *you* scared?" And then he asked to be left alone in his office.

But the threat was no longer limited to the Basha. Now I was being threatened along with him. I had gotten very close to the imminent danger facing him and had become, in a certain way, his accomplice.

I grew fed up with what was happening.

Even my relationship with my wife and my children wasn't what it used to be. I'd become quick to anger, which was unlike me. And I no longer had time to devote to them. Rasha kept on asking me what was going on with me, and whether I'd had a disagreement with the Basha, and I would say no, it was just that the Basha's business dealings had increased and the complications had increased along with them. And I'd explain to her what kinds of accounting tasks and business meetings were required of me, and whatever other lies I could come up with.

But I had no reason to think she had been convinced by anything I said to her.

I was not convincing, not in terms of the expressions I used, nor the tone of my voice, and certainly not in the way my eyes shifted all over the place. And I thought my facial expressions must have given me away, and led her to say, "A liar has to have a very good memory."

"What do you mean by that, Rasha?" I asked in anger.

"Two days ago," she answered, "you told me what was bothering you were demonstrations that were going to mess up the country, and the reason you were so busy was that you were making preparations to receive an important dignitary coming from Russia, and today . . ."

"Rasha," I said, interrupting her nervously, "can you please leave me alone and quit meddling in my business?"

## Samah Shahadeh

I was surprised to discover there was new security in place at our house, though I had no idea why.

It was no longer those clean-shaven men with the fine suits who used to come to our house. Fawaz had become even more inscrutable than before.

They installed cement barriers several meters past the entrance gate and the fence, and the number of guards increased to six – two of them patrolled the roof, each with a weapon in hand, two of them stood at the gate, one stood guard in a position near the fence and the remaining one patrolled the garden with a rifle and a revolver dangling from his belt.

Security measures meant the presence of imminent danger.

But the greater danger was the fact that I was no longer capable of understanding what was going on.

The situation could be more dangerous than I'd imagined, and Fawaz said nothing to me to ease my fears.

I felt trapped. My movements about the house and the garden were no longer free like before. What my father had said to me was true; there was something depriving me of sleep even in my own home. I wasn't even reading every morning like I used to, and no longer swam in the pool that was now in view of the two guards on the roof.

I asked myself whether the Arab Spring had reached us. Had this caused Fawaz to take all these precautions?

Although I rarely joined Fawaz in listening to all the clamor on satellite television in the living room, I decided that while I was waiting for the barbers to finish cutting his hair, giving him a shave, and clipping his fingernails and toenails down in the fitness room on the bottom floor of the house – activities that lasted a good two hours – I would immerse myself in watching all the international satellite stations he always followed: CNN, BBC, Al-Jazeera, French TV, Alhurra TV, Al Arabiya, Russia Today . . .

I got a headache and nearly got lost. Each channel had its own language, commentary, analysis, and news that it focused on, exclusively.

I felt bored, but it was more a feeling of listless apprehension than true boredom. I put on some clothes and got into my car, trying to escape that feeling of apprehension and also wanting to go out into the streets and find out if other people were bolstering the security around their homes like us, or at least see if there was anything in the streets and the squares that warranted taking safety measures.

I drove down the wide street leading to Al-Madina al-Tibbiya street, passed through the eight circles, arriving at First Circle near downtown.

There was nothing at all worth noting.

I decided to sit down at one of the First Circle cafés and have some ice cream, so I could watch what people were up to.

Everything was normal.

Young men and women were sitting around tables, talking and laughing. Others walked past each other without a care. There was no cause for alarm whatsoever.

So then why all the security outside our house where there were no people?

I went back home. Fawaz had a whole new appearance – a clean shave, short haircut, clipped and filed nails with the skin below all pink and healthy, and he was sporting a pair of eyeglasses his doctor prescribed for him after he complained he couldn't see the TV screen clearly.

I gave him a piece of my mind. He interrupted me, saying, "I haven't wanted to tell you what was going on with me for some time, in order not to worry you. But if you insist on knowing everything, I've received information that I am being targeted by terrorists."

"So then some of what Uroub predicted has come true," I said.

"God knows," he answered. "But I have to take precautions."

He didn't tell me why they were targeting him of all people. Was it because of his financial dealings, or was he involved in things I didn't know about?

I asked Sari and he confirmed what Fawaz said. Despite my being struck with fear about what might happen, I felt somewhat relieved inside. If this was what he had been hiding from me these past weeks, then he did so for fear of worrying me, not because there was another woman.

That relief I felt revealed the relative importance of things and events in my estimation – another woman in Fawaz's life was a greater danger than his being targeted by terrorists.

That was what I felt at the time.

But something bothered me when I saw Fawaz with his short haircut – which was that his once ruddy face was now quite pale. I asked him why he looked so pale and he said, "Have you forgotten I've been a vegetarian ever since I got back from Mumbai?"

"Do all vegetarians get like that?" I asked.

"Most of them."

I was not very convinced by what he said.

The next day I called Sari's wife, since she was the nutrition expert I had hired to provide his dietary program ever since he became a vegetarian. She confirmed what he said and she also added, "For this to happen to the Basha is understandable, because he's become a vegetarian, but what I don't understand is Sari losing five kilos since coming back from Mumbai without having become a vegetarian like the Basha. Didn't you notice that?"

## Sari Abu Amineh

When I called Darrar he said, "Soon I will be with Sharhabil and everything will be as you wish, God permitting."

"I think you've told me that before," I complained.

He was quiet and then said, "Put your trust in God. Soon you will hear news of our great victory, God willing."

"Yes, by the grace of God. I will wait."

I got the feeling from his tone of voice that he had some new information about Walid.

Darrar had a deep voice despite being so skinny, as if his throat were wider than other people's.

I didn't disclose anything to the Basha, because I wasn't certain of any of it, and besides, I didn't want to remind him of what he was trying to forget, even if only temporarily.

Mrs Samah was not doing well. Anxiety was all over her eyes and every feature of her face. She asked me who wanted to kill the Basha. That was the first time she asked me this kind of question.

Her questions had always revealed her fear that something was being hidden from her. This time she asked me directly about the danger. And her tone was unfamiliar to me; it seemed to express a loss of patience.

"Mrs Samah," I said, "who would target the Basha other than the terrorists scattered all over Afghanistan and Libya and Syria and Iraq, who might be headed our way?"

"Why him in particular?" she asked.

"I'm like you," I answered. "I ask myself the same question."

Before she could say anything further the maid came to inform me the Basha wanted to see me in his office. It was perfect timing. I let out a heavy sigh and excused myself.

The Basha told me he was no longer comfortable with the whole situation and ordered me to go back to Umm al-Walid to get new information on her son.

I thought he must have known that my going to see Umm al-Walid wasn't going to get us anywhere, but he wanted to do something. He wanted me to do something, anything.

This time I felt there was a look in his eyes that cried out for help.

"Before I go back to her," I said, "I'm going to check the airport logs and the border crossings. Maybe he entered legally."

"Don't bother," he said. "Chances are he got smuggled in somehow."

## Darrar al-Ghoury

I found out that the reason for Sharhabil's disappearance was that he joined the mujahideen in Syria. That information shook my original deduction that the intelligence services were after him because of the danger he posed to the Americans, because the Americans hadn't entered Syria. So then why did Sari want to get rid of him?

I signed up on the list of fighters wanting to transfer to Syria after they announced opening the doors of jihad there. Maybe I would come across Sharhabil once again.

I asked myself why would I want to follow him all the way to Syria, after having been given the chance to do the job I came to Afghanistan for but didn't do anything about.

Then it occurred to me that I wasn't thinking about my family like I had been at first. I felt what was happening to me had created a kind of harshness that was strange to me, a harshness towards my family and my acquaintances, towards everything that connected me to my country.

All that mattered to me now was getting to Syria and finding Sharhabil, not only so I could carry out my mission with him, but because having him within reach made me feel safe.

## Muntaha al-Rayyeh

I said to myself: What if Fawaz al-Shardah or that Sari character sent some sort of information to al-Walid, telling him he was an illegitimate child?

Al-Walid never contacted me except that one time, after Nael, Abu al-Walid died, and even then he was hesitant. Could he have received information about his origins and about his real father?

That would have been a disaster.

Sari gave me his phone number and told me to call him if necessary. But I would certainly not call.

My concerns grew. It was as though I couldn't escape my past.

I went to see Sheikh Abu Muhsin, the imam of the mosque who knew al-Walid before he left and knew Nael before he died. I thought he might be close to the mujahideen.

He was standing on the stairs at the entrance to the mosque wearing his lead-gray *dishdasha* robe that was the same color as his long, unkempt beard.

He looked me in the face. His stare was not very friendly.

He shook his head asking God for forgiveness and lowered his eyes.

I asked him how I could get in touch with al-Walid and find out if he was OK.

"Dear sister," he said, fiddling with his beard, "Al-Walid has gone to do jihad for the sake of God, according to my knowledge.

Take joy in this, and wish for him to attain martyrdom, with God's permission."

"Wish for his death, sheikh?!" I said with disapproval.

With disdain, he replied, "The pleasant life is in Eternal Paradise, with the prophets and the righteous and the martyrs. Or do you prefer this transitory life to the eternal hereafter?"

"Fine," I said. "Can't you tell him through one of your sheikh acquaintances to contact me, even just for one minute, or give me his phone number if he has a phone? I am his mother who gave birth to him, after all. Don't I have the right to hear his voice before something bad happens to him, God forbid?"

"Something bad?" he screamed, angrily. "Are you calling martyrdom for the sake of God something bad? This is indeed the vilest sort of blasphemy, woman!"

I was confused. I felt we were both having problems with our wording, and with the manner of the questions and the answers.

"Forgive me, sheikh," I said. "I am a mother, and it seems my longing to see my son has made me forget how to speak to you. Or maybe I . . ."

And when my tongue got tied as I tried to finish my sentence, he decided to finish it his own way. "Or maybe you are like all women – lacking in brains and religion."

With much displeasure I said, "Couldn't you find a better way than that to respond to the mother of one of your glorified mujahideen? Truly, the meaning of words is found in how they are expressed."

Then I turned angrily to go home and almost bumped into a bearded sheikh who was very small in stature and was coming up the stairs towards Sheikh Abu Muhsin. Our eyes met for a moment before we looked away.

That sheikh was familiar to me. I had seen him before.

I started to worry. I felt that sheikh, who wore a white *kufiyyeh* headscarf with black *agal* cord and let his beard grow freely, was not just a passerby I happened to run into by accident. Something inside me pushed me to remember who he was. Where had I seen him? When? And why did I feel the necessity to remember him?

After that encounter I felt afraid. If that was those sheikhs' way of responding to a woman like myself, who wore a scarf over her hair and dressed in modest clothing, and asked about her son the mujahid, then what would they do if they were to discover my secret?

## Abu Hudhayfah

A few weeks after settling into our base north of Deir al-Zor, our group leader was transferred and Sharhabil was promoted to commander of the Suqur al-Duru' group in the camp. I thought it was a well-deserved promotion. Commander Al-Thuqafy had recommended him to two members of the high command after Sharhabil destroyed an armored vehicle during our assault on an advanced position of the Syrian regime's troops west of Sahl al-Ghab.

Another matter cropped up a few weeks after we moved to Syria. The medic Darrar al-Ghoury joined up with us, along with a band of mujahideen who came to assist their brothers after the doors of jihad in Syria were opened.

I took a liking to that medic; he was dear to my heart and to Sharhabil's heart, too. It reached the point where we formed a three-way bond of mutual love and understanding.

Darrar told me all about his village in the Jordan Valley. He said it was just a few kilometers from the Jordan River, within walking distance. I marveled at this: Seeing as the Jewish soldiers were within range of rifle fire, canons, rockets, and even slingshots, why not open the doors to jihad from there, considering it would be so easy?

"Isn't there someone carrying out attacks on the Jewish soldiers west of the river?" I asked.

"That's difficult, Abu Hudhayfah," he said. "Because the Jordanian authorities won't allow people near it."

"Since when?" I asked. "And in which corner of the earth has it ever been allowed for us to carry out jihad, Darrar? Jihad is taken by force. It is forced upon the ruling authorities and the people. If a hand's span of Muslim ground is occupied by the enemy, then jihad becomes our religious duty."

Before I could finish that last statement, Commander Al-Thuqafi's car, a Toyota SUV we captured from laymen with the Free Army during one of our battles with them, entered the compound.

Commander Al-Thuqafi, who had been driving the car himself, got out from the driver's side, and then Sharhabil descended from the other door on the passenger side of the car.

In recent days I noticed Al-Thuqafi had Sharhabil in the car with him on three occasions. When I asked him about this new development, he merely said, "Jihadi matters, Abu Hudhayfah."

## Sari Abu Amineh

I wasn't expecting the heightened security that had been placed all about the Basha's home without my knowledge.

It came as a surprise to me, but I didn't dare ask the Basha about it at all. I knew where to draw the line when it came to matters of his that he did not want to tell me about. Rather than asking him any questions, I gave my vote of confidence for taking this precautionary step, and added, "It's necessary and the timing is good."

Earlier, I had carried out the Basha's instructions and gone with a man with an olive complexion, tall stature, a handle-bar mustache and rough hands named Abu Khalaf. I found out he was a former military officer who had retired a few years earlier.

We went in a small truck to an open and deserted area west of Wadi al-Sayr, and there he taught me how to use a short pistol. It was a 9 mm Star model. I was beset with conflicting emotions while shooting bullets at a metal target that took me thirty-seven tries to finally hit.

That was not all. He also explained about developing a "security sense" and the various stages of it, and about signs of danger and their potentialities. He talked about how to anticipate attacks before they happened, and about the traits of combatants and assailants and their speech patterns. Before giving me the pistol and its leather holster, he taught me how to hang it under my armpit, how to draw it and how to engage it easily and quickly. Then he took me back to the Basha's house.

I never thought I'd become one of those people who carried guns. After all, I was a man who did work that required thinking and management skills, which were far removed from violence. That was how it should be.

However, as long as I'd come close to the hyenas, I might as well have my hatchet with me, as they say.

Rasha eventually noticed the pistol, and made her astonishment and horror over what was happening to me very clear. I didn't know what else to tell her except that guns had become a required part of the job these days.

"That must mean you're going to war at work," she said.

"Exactly," I said with annoyance. Then I added, "Life itself is a kind of war."

Once again I called Darrar. He was my only access to information at the time. He told me that Walid had gone for jihad in Syria and no place else. I was relieved for a while; at least he hadn't come to Amman as I had feared.

Then he told me that their leadership in Afghanistan had opened the jihad market in Syria. He used the phrase "jihad market," which was the first time I'd ever heard that expression.

He also told me that he had signed himself up to go there, and he promised I would be the first to know what happened to him when he arrived.

I rubbed my hands together and called the Basha in order to tell him the good news. But he was distressed and couldn't speak. I wondered what was going on with the Basha.

# Samah Shahadeh

My father came to our house.

He didn't come alone. He was accompanied by two black Jeeps – one in front of his car and the other behind. Each one had three armed security guards inside.

Why was he keeping all that security?

I sat with him in the garden, next to the *houri* fountain, while his bodyguards scrutinized our security guards positioned up on the roof and in and outside the garden. I saw them pointing at more than one location inside the house and outside it, discussing matters amongst themselves.

"If a person has more than a one percent chance his life is in danger," he said, "then what is better? To ignore this possibility, or prepare for it?" Then he added, "What scares me is that one percent."

"What has brought this on?" I asked.

He said in a very mechanical tone devoid of emotion, "Fawaz might die at any moment. They have made a threat on him. I believe the threats of those people."

"What people?" I asked, angrily.

"The ones who want to kill him, Samah," he answered.

It seemed to me that even my father could not understand. I didn't get anything out of him, despite all my schemes and attempts to take advantage of his sound judgment.

But I felt certain he was hiding something from me. Even the way he talked about Fawaz being targeted didn't match how one might expect someone to talk about such a thing.

"OK," I said. "I understand Fawaz is being threatened and therefore is taking necessary precautions, but why are you going overboard with precautions for yourself?"

Instead of answering, he asked, "Where is Fawaz?"

"He left an hour ago," I said. "Didn't you tell him you were coming?"

"No," he answered. Then, while looking at his guards who had now come closer to us, he said, "I have an appointment I must go to now."

Before getting up to leave, he looked at my face and shook his head, saying, "I thought you were a lot smarter than you are."

Then he got up and walked over to his driver and his group of bodyguards.

Before he got too far away, I asked, "Why did you say that?"

He turned around and just winked at me, one of those fatherly winks he cast my way ever since I was a child, whenever I failed to grasp the implications of what he said. But this time it was different. He was slower than I had been accustomed to.

His eyelids were droopy.

# Sari Abu Amineh

I went to the Basha's office.

He was relaxing on an upholstered chair with two armrests and footrests. His appearance showed clear signs of the onset of old age, especially when I noticed the bags under his eyes and the protruding veins on the yellow patches of skin on his legs which were raised up on the footrests, and the sparse white hairs growing on his knuckles.

He listened to me with little concern and then said, while shaking his knees, "This means that Uroub's prophecy will come true."

"I really don't know, Basha," I said. "Only God knows why the world changed this way ever since we saw that fortune-teller."

"Where is the picture of Walid?" he asked.

I showed it to him on my cell phone. He looked at it and then reached into one of his desk drawers. He opened it and took out a photograph, handed it to me, and said, "This is him at age twenty. I got hold of it my own way."

"That's him," I said hastily, "with his long hair, but without a beard."

"Take a good look at the picture," he said.

I looked more carefully. All the features resembled the Basha: the brown eyes, the thick eyebrows, the hooked nose.

"Don't you think I resemble him?"

I was taken aback. "Isn't that a picture of Walid?" I asked.

"It's a picture of me when I was his age," he said.

Oh God! I felt like such a failure for not having recognized the Basha's test.

"Forgive me, Basha," I said. "Things just aren't as they used to be. People and events have all become one big surprise. I feel like I'm living in a strange and incomprehensible era." Then I added, "If you decide we should bring him here instead of getting rid of him, I will arrange it."

He sighed and said, "It's too late."

# Darrar al-Ghoury

I understood from the last phone call I received from Sari that he had sent a messenger to my family in Mashari'. He gave them 500 dinars and told them I had sent it.

It seems that that sly fox realized they wouldn't question how a mujahid fighting for the sake of God could send money to his family while he was in the midst of battle. Considering how desperately they ran after even a single dinar, I could only imagine what my father would do when handed 500 dinars all at once.

Sari told me – also – that time was running out. Then he asked me, "Haven't you had the opportunity to carry out what we agreed on yet?"

I told him that the mujahideen hadn't given me the chance to get Sharhabil alone, and plus he had been leaving the camp quite a bit.

He was silent at first and then he said, in a tone that wavered between anxious and angry, "Where? Where does he go?"

"No one knows," I said. "Not even his closest friends."

He was silent again. Then he said, "But he comes back to your camp in the end, doesn't he?"

"Absolutely," I answered.

As if making a threat Sari said, "You had better finish with the matter quickly."

Despite the threats contained in that phone call, it strengthened my resolve and pushed me to do what I was sent to do.

Commander Al-Thuqafy, along with three groups of fighters and their commanders, had embarked upon a violent confrontation with Syrian regime forces who had succeeded in taking two of our hideouts in south Deir al-Zor a few days earlier.

The sun had disappeared behind the sharp hills and the only people left in the tents and trenches of the camp were fifteen wounded men I was treating and trying to comfort. Sharhabil had returned with his jihadi battalion from another combat mission that consisted of eight hours of attacking and retreating.

The members of the battalion went straight to their tents to sleep without having anything to eat first. They were exhausted.

Sharhabil had a superficial wound on his side, so I treated it with iodine and bandaged it up. He found a spot for himself and fell asleep on a mat of indeterminate color.

I heard him snoring a few minutes later, despite the sounds of distant gunfire and explosions.

I covered him with a blanket and looked closely at his face as best I could by the faint twinkle of starlight.

He had surrendered completely into a peaceful slumber. His sweat smelled like that of a tiger having returned from a perilous hunt. There had been some salt crystals in his hair and beard that I brushed off when I was treating his wound.

I thought: Sharhabil's death would mean a life and a future for me, and keeping him alive might mean my being found out and put to death.

I had only one solution before me: to do away with him by injecting him with an overdose of drugs that would kill him. It would be easy for him and easy for me, and when Al-Thuqafy and the other mujahideen came back, they would think he died from his wound.

Glory to You, my Creator. You have dominion and power over everything.

What was I to do?

This was the first time I felt that I – after Almighty God – was to decide whether a man sleeping right there in front of me would live or die. It was a feeling that sparked the mind, heated the body, wrenched the heart and conjured bitter weeping over the difficult choices one faced in this mortal life.

Without meaning to, I cleared my throat and Sharhabil woke up. He reached to feel his wound.

I shook my head in dismay and sighed.

I wished I could understand why that cursed Sari wanted to get rid of Sharhabil. No doubt there was a big secret lurking beneath it all that only he and God Almighty knew.

Sharhabil asked for a cup of water, so I gave him a little sip with my own hands. He asked me if Commander Al-Thuqafy had returned yet, so I asked him to pray for his courageous victory.

He prayed for him and for the path of the mujahideen to be victorious. Then he got up to relieve himself.

I thought about asking him if he knew of someone in Amman named Sari, but I changed my mind, because a direct question might cause alarm. It would be better to try a different approach.

When he came back, I started talking about my folks in Mashari' and about Amman and the people's lack of religion there. I mentioned the many shops that sold alcohol and all the unveiled women, and the corruption. I told him about a man from Amman who married the daughter of a citrus fruit grocer two days before I left Mashari'. He had a big wedding and invited dignitaries from Amman and from the Jordan Valley.

I kept quiet for a little while and then to test his reaction on hearing the name I said, "I remember his name was Sari. Yes, I think it was Sari."

There was no surprise reaction from Sharhabil. He went back to the mat and fell back asleep.

I had a long night. I took a walk a short distance away from him. Then I heard the sound of an explosion that shook the ground, causing Sharhabil to wake up and start reciting the *shahada* in a loud voice.

How amazing is man, whose inner secrets are known only to the Lord of Creation. In spite of what I had intended to do to Sharhabil, I felt as though a heavy burden had been lifted off my chest when he was startled from his sleep at that merciful moment.

# Abu Hudhayfah

It was a pitch-dark night and I was feeling pessimistic for some reason.

We lit a fire and gathered around it.

A few minutes later, Commander Al-Thuqafy stood up and took Sharhabil by the hand. Sharhabil got up and they headed to his tent without saying a word.

An hour later I got a call from my wife's brother Saleh telling me she had suffered a stroke.

He said to me, using my real name – Hatem – that it would be best for me to see her before God took His precious gift from her body.

Of course I knew it was merely a trick that Saleh – who I didn't trust for a second – was resorting to in an attempt to dissuade me from carrying out jihad for the sake of God, and lure me back to my village in Asir.

"She has God with her, Saleh. He is of great mercy," I said. "But I cannot come and do not want to come, either."

"If you wish to return," he said, "I can make all the arrangements for you to enter the country, with the government's knowledge, and without your getting hurt. Your country is your 'priority,' Hatem."

"Jihad for the sake of God has the highest priority, more than any country," I said. "Leave the governments to themselves, Saleh, and go back to your religion. Maybe God will enlighten your heart and guide you onto the straight path."

"May God guide you, Hatem," he replied, "and put you in your right mind. What shall I tell your wife if she comes out of her coma?"

"To pray to her Lord from dawn to dusk. Perhaps He will see her troubles and heal her."

Sharhabil rejoined us. I didn't ask about what was going on between him and Commander Al-Thuqafy, for on previous similar occasions I had asked and gotten no answer.

I called my wife in order to confirm what her brother had told me about her, and he answered the phone instead of her. He said she hadn't regained consciousness yet and finished by saying, "You'd better come back quickly so you can see her before she parts from this life, God forbid."

"Stop lying, Saleh. Aren't you ever going to change? Haven't you come to your senses and learned to be truthful?"

"Listen, Hatem," he said. "May God give you long life. It's true that a man's lifespan is in God's hands, but the doctors are saying she will not live more than a few days. If you hear news of her death in a day or so, then don't blame me. The messenger's duty is to convey the message."

Saleh succeeded in making me believe that my wife was in the throes of death. I did indeed believe him despite the fact I didn't trust him.

The bundles of firewood were ablaze, and a large number of mujahideen had gathered around, among them Darrar. The flames and sparks of the fire glowed against their faces and the machine guns they had strapped to themselves while they talked optimistically about the future of Islam and the Muslim lands.

I wondered to myself whether my wife would die before I had a chance to see her.

I remembered when she came to me as a shy bride in all her virtue and timidity, and committed herself to me according to the

Law of God and His noble Prophet, thus becoming my dwelling place in the world. I abandoned her to follow the call to jihad for the sake of God less than a year after our marriage, and all she could bring herself to say was that she would wait for me to return safe and sound, God willing.

A man's lifespan is in the hands of God Almighty, but I just couldn't believe that my wife who was barely twenty-six years old, had suffered a stroke – the kind of thing that usually afflicted the elderly, not the young.

I kept my secret to myself and didn't tell any of my mujahideen brothers about it, especially since my brother-in-law might be a worthless liar.

The next day after we finished eating breakfast, I sat with Sharhabil on a couple of sheepskins under a shady tree at the southern edge of the camp, until it was time for him to leave on another mission whose contents and whereabouts he didn't disclose to me. It seemed to be one of high importance.

While we were in the midst of reminiscing about our brothers who had been martyred and had left this life, my cell phone suddenly rang. That ring was more like an alarm system connected right to my heart. I checked the number and it was Saleh. I picked up immediately.

His voice was strained and sad, and I could hear the din of people around him and the sound of someone reciting the Quran in the background.

"God rest her soul," he said. "And may you be granted a long life after her."

I hung up the phone and burst into tears.

Yes, by God, I wept like no man has ever wept before. Tears streamed down my face and mingled with my saliva and the dirt. Sharhabil consoled me and lessened my distress with comforting words and verses from the Quran calling one to submit to God's will and divine decree. But in his eyes I could see restrained tears.

He was quiet for a while and then he said, "Strangers, Abu Hudhayfah . . . We came into this world as strangers, and we leave it and our loved ones leave it as strangers. So why this grief, which weakens the heart and the mind and undermines the determination of the mujahid?"

Then he headed towards a car that had entered the camp. He got in and sped away.

My brothers in the camp came to me and offered their condolences. They spoke heartfelt words that helped calm my soul. They told me about dear ones who had passed away in their absence – mothers, fathers, children, brothers, and sisters.

I calmed down a little, but the ghost of my wife continued to haunt me after that. At times I would hear her inciting me to fight for the sake of God, and other times I would hear her blaming me for abandoning her.

Darrar al-Ghoury came to me late at night. He had gone by motorcycle to a nearby hideout to treat some wounded mujahideen there.

He consoled me and offered fervent condolences for my loss. Then he asked me about Sharhabil, who he loved like a brother. When I told him that a car had come, picked him up and sped off with him, he appeared worried. He asked if he was going to be gone long.

Darrar, God bless him, loved Sharhabil very much. But I noticed that maybe he was a bit more interested in him than was necessary.

## Sari Abu Amineh

I received three strange photos from Darrar, with no explanation: one of chunks of flesh that made me want to vomit, one of pools of blood, and one of the remnants of the mangled car.

I didn't understand any of it.

I called him and he said, "That's all that's left of the target al-Walid. He carried out a suicide mission, may God have mercy on his soul. I was the one who encouraged him to do it."

It was ten o'clock at night. Even though it wasn't the proper time to visit the Basha or to speak with him, I called him, filled with excitement. "I have some big news. It would be best if I came to see you in person."

He was silent at first and then said, "Come over."

On my way over, some devilish thoughts crossed my mind about that wretch Darrar. And about my success in diverting the course of fate.

I went to the Basha and found him sitting alone in an armchair in his office, wearing a blue robe over white silk pajamas. Between his fingers was a fat cigar about half-way consumed.

The office was filled with the smell of tobacco. The Basha had dark circles around his eyes that I hadn't noticed before. Quiet flute music played in the background.

"Walid is dead, Basha," I said.

His eyes widened and he raised his thick eyebrows. "Are you sure?"

"Of course," I said. I showed him the photos I had received from Darrar. "This is what's left of him, Basha. There is nothing to worry about anymore."

He inspected the pictures and then sighed and said, "Who killed him?"

"He carried out a suicide mission," I said.

"And the man you sent, what did he do?" he asked.

"He's the one who arranged for the mission and encouraged him to do it."

He looked away from the photos and looked directly into my face. "And so we have defeated fate. The one at whose hands my demise was to come is now dead!"

"We should celebrate, Basha," I said. "We have all played a part in defeating fate."

But then he suddenly went silent, and signs of anxiety flashed across his face. Then as he blew out a puff of cigar smoke he said, "And what if his comrades are victorious in Syria?"

"God forbid, Basha."

The tone of his voice did not betray much joy or delight at the death of Walid. It was idle, not pleased, and not pleasing either. It was not at a level proportionate to the significant news I had given him.

After a contemplative pause he said, "It makes me happy that I was able to change fate, and it bothers me that for thirty years I was unable to search for Walid. To buy him, for example."

"You didn't know he existed, Basha," I said.

"Because I didn't follow my instincts like I always do!"

# Darrar al-Ghoury

A few days after inventing the story of Sharhabil's martyrdom and getting Sari to believe it, the mujahideen left camp to confront Syrian government soldiers who had overtaken villages in the western sector.

They chose to do a surprise attack on those soldiers at night, aided by mujahideen from other bases. This was because the government soldiers were able to reach the western sector, which posed a direct threat to our encampment and to all of the nearby hideouts, according to Commander Al-Thuqafy's early morning speech to 200 mujahideen.

As he spoke Al-Thuqafy had girded himself with his belt of explosives and was wearing a specked black *kufiyyeh* scarf that was tightly wrapped around his head and connected with his black beard. He was holding a cloak in his hands the color of dirt that was stained with dry blood. He stood up on a boulder overlooking the crowded assembly of mujahideen with their weapons, and delivered his effective speech, which he began by saying, "O mujahideen, union of troops who have vanquished the heretics and the secularists . . . O tower around which have gathered the infidels and the nonbelievers, the Nusairis and the Safavids, the Persians, the Arabs, the white, the red, the brown, and the black, and all the devils of the earth. O you traversers of lands and gulfs and continents who are impeded by nothing and are stopped by no one. O you who have increased in number in the mountain paths of God, and His seas, and His skies which He has opened to you and whose gateways He has widened for you, without anyone knowing the secret of your patience and perseverance and triumph but Almighty God . . ."

Then he began to incite the fervor of the mujahideen, talking about the gratification of victory over the infidels, about the true goal of the mujahid, which is martyrdom for the sake of God, where one finds that Paradise God promised to the mujahideen, with its wide-eyed *houris*, full-bosomed beauties, who neither menstruate nor give birth, with no mucus nor saliva, no defect and no impurity . . . beauties among the most perfect of God's creations."

Then he raised the cloak he was holding in his right hand, saying, "You all know Abu Junayd, who was martyred three months ago during our raid on the passport offices, may God have mercy on his soul and let him enter His spacious Paradise. Abu Junayd was the grandson of the great mujahid Al-Amir Abd al-Qadir al-Jaza'iry, and his heroic deeds we will never forget as long as we live. This is his cloak, stained with his blood . . . the cloak of Abu Junayd."

Then he took a big whiff of it and breathed in its smell before us.

"By God, the musky fragrance of his blood still fills the air ninety days after his martyrdom. And this is just one of the miracles of God the Mighty, the Sublime. By God, the white dove almost never leaves his graveside in the village of Al-Jalaa which God blessed with the opportunity to embrace his pure body."

Then he pointed to one of the mujahideen, approached him, handed the cloak to him, and asked him to take it around to show all the others, who breathed in its smell, one after the other, and shook their heads with emotion.

The voices of the mujahideen rose up and grew louder. Their voices were interconnected and bolstered one another, and the way they enunciated inspired strength and resolve into each other's hearts and souls.

When darkness fell, everyone had left the camp. Only four guards remained at the main entrance to the camp, and a number of guards on the edges, in addition to fifteen wounded men in the trenches and the tents.

While I was in the midst of examining the wounded, I heard the sound of a man moaning and groaning in pain coming from the direction of one of the tents. I walked towards the sound and found a mass of some sort wrapped in a blanket on the gravel. I hadn't seen the thing before. I went closer to it, attempting to get a better look under the light of my little flashlight, when suddenly the blanket opened and whoever was inside fired three shots at my chest and my head using a revolver with a silencer on it. I fell to the ground and the shooter got up out of the blanket and took off.

I screamed and reached to feel the top of my head and my chest. I could feel the hot flow of my blood. I heard the voice of one of the camp guards calling to me and then I passed out.

# Samah Shahadeh

I suggested to Fawaz that we get away from it all for a while, take a trip for a week or two until things calmed down and the threat on him that he talked about had passed. It had been months since we'd traveled together. As he put his eyeglasses on and adjusted them, he answered, "How can I leave my work in this kind of atmosphere?"

"If you're under threat, what choice would you make – your business interests or your life?" I asked.

"Of course I choose life," he answered. "But this life of ours is tied to our interests!"

Maybe he was right. Fawaz had dedicated more than thirty-three years of his life to reach where he'd gotten. He embarked on risky ventures, and faced numerous schemes from his competitors and those who envied him, who teamed up against him more than once, and nearly ruined his relationship with two of the most prominent figures in the country, thanks to their craftily constructed plots. He even told me one time that they delivered a report to the prime minister and others about a plan Fawaz supposedly had hatched for undermining the national economy, in cooperation with people with interests and organizations outside Jordan. A plan that – according to their report – rested on inciting international and local entities to force the central bank and those in charge to unpeg the dinar from the dollar, and peg it instead to a basket of currencies. According to the supposed plan, Fawaz would profit from the new exchange rate and insider trading during the chaotic transitional phase which usually accompanies currency fluctuations.

That report received a lot of attention, because Fawaz was well-known for his far-reaching relationships inside and outside the country, in addition to owning numerous currency exchange offices which could profit a great deal from such a transformation if it were to occur.

However, Fawaz was very strong in his position.

Actually, he became strong after my father stepped in, in his inspired way – from a distance, but with amazing efficacy.

My father didn't like traditional methods. He dealt with problems like a skilled billiard player who aimed north in order to hit the south or the east or the west. When the report on Fawaz became known, my father made a public statement to one of the newspapers stating that he was in the process of hiring a research center to do a study on fraudulent reports being presented to the government, and to income taxes from agencies and companies and some individuals, and that he would be submitting the study with its supporting evidence to the audit office, free of charge, as a service to the national economy.

That was how he rescued Fawaz. Then he phoned me and said, "Tell Fawaz he should be able to sleep in peace now."

That public statement resulted in an instant change in the course of the attack on Fawaz. The report was considered "conspiratorial" and an attempt by those who had prepared it to create chaos in the country and defame the image of the national economy. Another fallout was the dismissal of the minister of finance and two higher-ups in the Central Bank.

We were sitting in the living room, Fawaz and I. His cell phone rang. The ring tone was an excerpt of a piece by Bach that I had picked out for him.

Fawaz had been obliged to familiarize himself with Beethoven and Mozart and Bizet and Bach, in order to make me feel he shared my interests. Music had not been on his list of interests when he married me.

He looked at the colorful screen of his cellphone and then headed out of the living room before starting his phone conversation in a hushed voice.

# Darrar al-Ghoury

I regained consciousness and found myself swimming in my own blood. I discovered my chest and head were wrapped in white bandages and tape, and there was a group of mujahideen congregated around me. Beside me was Abu Hudhayfah, and above my head stood Sharhabil, who kneeled down beside me the moment he saw me wake up, and grabbed and shook me.

"Tell me who did this to you!"

"It was very dark," I said in a feeble voice.

"Why don't you answer?" he said, agitated. "Who wanted to kill you?"

"I did answer you, Sharhabil," I said. "I didn't see his face because of the dark."

He looked at Abu Hudhayfah and said, "What's wrong with him? Why doesn't he answer?"

"He can't speak, Commander," he said. "It seems there's something wrong with his tongue, or the part of his brain that controls speech. That happened to one of the mujahideen in Afghanistan, and he got better, thank God."

Abu Hudhayfah calls Sharhabil "*commander*"? What about Al-Thuqafy? What happened while I was unconscious?

"What's with you?" I said. "I am speaking. Where is Commander Al-Thuqafy?"

They didn't seem to hear what I said.

I noticed that the way Sharhabil looked at me was different, as was the way he looked at the others. And he spoke sharply. His facial features seemed stern to me, too, far-removed from the patience that had characterized him in the past.

Sharhabil remained bewildered and unsettled. He started pacing and forming a tight fist with his right hand, then relaxing it. He stopped and put his index finger to his lips, thinking. Then he came back to me asking once again for details I didn't know. I wondered what had happened to warrant Sharhabil's interest in investigating me. And not only that; they also brought the camp security guards to him and he submitted them to a lengthy interrogation in front of me. Even the wounded were not exempted from his interrogations. He seemed more like someone who had gotten wind of a conspiracy. I heard him say as he shouted at them in a very stern voice, "What were you doing? How did he get into our camp and shoot Darrar without your nabbing him? Don't you know that dogs only enter through an open door? Why did you leave the borders of our camp open?"

Then he turned to me, peering with his angry eyes into mine, as though he wanted to read what was behind them, and asked me, "Why did they come after you, out of all the mujahideen?"

I smiled innocently. I was confident and coherent despite having lost the ability to speak. The attempt to kill me had really happened, no doubt about it, and if not for God's protection and mercy, the bullet would have pierced my heart and I'd be dead.

Maybe death would have been better. But I wasn't sure if such a death would be considered martyrdom.

## Muntaha al-Rayyeh

As I usually did when misfortunes arose and life became harsh for me, I went to visit my mother, hoping she had something to say that might comfort me.

Her face was tired, and her eyes were sunken into their sockets. Her voice came feebly from between her shriveled lips.

My father was in his bedroom, which he didn't leave except when absolutely necessary, due to his need for someone to lead him since losing his eyesight to diabetes. At any rate, he was far from being concerned with what was going on with me.

I made two cups of tea and sat down beside her. I told her what happened.

I didn't see anything in her eyes indicating she was the least bit moved by what I told her about Sari's visits and his having been sent by Fawaz al-Shardah and all his questions about al-Walid.

When she started talking, I felt she hadn't forgotten about what I did in Paris, despite the passing of so many years. But the way she addressed me had changed. Instead of getting worked up, she was calm, and sober, and wise. She said to me, "I expected this to happen one day, for the sin only dies when the sinner dies."

"But I have repented," I said. "Truly repented!"

She sighed. "Repentance is between you and God. As for sin, it follows its owner like a vicious shadow."

I became annoyed. "I came to you for help, not to be scolded!"

She looked into my eyes as if she wanted to crawl inside them and said, "You do not love al-Walid. Maybe you wish he would die."

She shocked me with that. "Would I wish for my own son, who I gave birth to, to die?!" I said in protest and disapproval. "Why would I?"

"Even if he did die, your sin will only die when you die," she said.

I calmed myself and said, "Fine. What should I do about this affliction named Sari?"

She answered after a pause, "Your husband is dead. Al-Walid is far away from you. Your father can't see. What is troubling you?"

I didn't receive one bit of comfort from what she said, and when I said goodbye and was on my way out, I heard her say, "If that fellow Sari comes back, call the police."

Sometimes I experienced incidents I could not understand or explain, and they complicated my problems even more. When my mother uttered the word "police," the image of that sheikh I had seen on the steps of the mosque with Sheikh Abu Muhsin popped into my mind – the short sheikh with the beard and the white head wrap.

Once again I had the feeling it wasn't just some passerby I had seen at the door to the mosque. He was part of some bigger story.

So who was he?

## Abu Hudhayfah

This is your will, Lord of the Worlds. To You belongs praise and gratitude. And You are the master over all things.

During our raid on the western sector, in which we confronted the Syrian regime soldiers, Commander Al-Thuqafy was martyred.

Glory to God. The eloquent speech he gave before we set out for the western sector was his last speech in this world.

What pained me was that we were unable to retrieve his pure body and bring it back with us when we withdrew, for he was martyred deep inside a congregation of enemy tanks – he and nine of the mujahideen he chose to accompany him in the front line. The regime forces closed in on them and got the better of them after the mujahideen killed several of the enemy in that violent and vicious battle.

Even though I envied him the blessing of martyrdom, I felt the major loss we suffered as a result. He was our chief commander, after all, who directed our incursions, and the one who negotiated our relationship with the high command, and from whom we derived strength, determination, and fortitude.

But God the Almighty chose him to be by His side, and there is no complaint against the judgment of God, who is most glorious.

When we returned to our camp, the unexpected happened. The car of the financial officer, who came by about once a month, entered the camp, followed by the car of one of the high commanders, which also had three masked men inside. Sharhabil and three leaders from the jihadi groups in the camps were waiting for them. They all went together to the tent of the martyr Al-Thuqafy, entered it, and closed themselves inside.

The other matter that threw me off balance was that before we got back to the camp, the mujahid Darrar al-Ghoury had been the target of an assassination attempt that he barely survived. And he lost his ability to speak as a result.

They finished their meeting and came out of the tent. We were all congregated around Darrar al-Ghoury. The financial officer stood among us and asked for God's mercy for our great martyr Al-Thuqafy and for all of our martyrs. Then one of the masked men by the name of Abu Ibada came forward, announcing that he had come as a representative of the high command. Abu Ibada began talking without removing the covering over his mouth. He praised God for His judgment, and for His choice, which fell upon one of our noblest leaders on the battlefield. Then he reminded us of the unlawfulness of *salat al-janaza* (burial prayers) or *al-gha'ib* (*in absentia* prayers) for the martyr killed by the infidels, because our noble Prophet ordered the martyrs of the Battle of Uhud to be buried in their blood; He did not wash them or pray over them.

After Abu Ibada recited the *fatiha* for the souls of our martyrs, while we silently recited it along with him, he said that our high commanders were in a constant state of vigilance over our battle against falsehood, and that they assigned as replacement for any commander a host of new commanders from among the best mujahideen. He promised God to avenge the martyr Commander Al-Thuqafy and the rest of our martyrs. Then Abu Ibada said that the leadership of the camp had now been entrusted to the mujahid Sharhabil, based on an emergency decision taken by the high command immediately upon hearing the news of Al-Thuqafy's martyrdom.

His voice was muffled because of the mask, but I heard everything he said. I felt comfortable with their choice of Sharhabil as commander of our camp, so I approached him and gave him a congratulatory embrace. And everyone else did the same.

Sharhabil seemed different this time. He stood up straight, and the features of his face were missing their familiar shadows, making him appear serious and tense, especially when he carried out his interrogation of what happened with Darrar.

# Darrar al-Ghoury

My wounds healed and I recovered my ability to speak, with God's help, so I thanked my Lord, and performed two prostrations, praising Him for the blessing of healing.

I learned that Sharhabil had become the camp's commander, and I remembered that wretch Sari. All my worries and doubts came back to me.

Certainly Sari was the one who'd sent that conspirator to kill me. I no longer had any doubt.

Maybe he found out that Sharhabil had not been martyred, that I had lied to him and failed to carry out my mission, and so he wanted to get rid of me.

Sari had a very long reach. I certainly was in the best position to know that. And it wasn't far-fetched for him to find out I hadn't died and send someone to try to kill me again. Then again, it would have been possible for whoever tried to kill me to kill Sharhabil; he was Sari's real target, not me.

I thought and thought, and then an idea flashed in my mind like a bolt of lightning: Sari believed Sharhabil was dead and now he wanted to get rid of me in order to cover his tracks.

Either way, Sari wanted to kill me – whether I killed Sharhabil or not.

How wicked was that creature! How vile!

I no longer had a place among the mujahideen. At any moment Sari could betray me in his way, or send someone to kill me. And besides, I wanted to escape these straits I had put myself in; I was neither with the mujahideen in heart and soul, nor was I against them. O God! How difficult was my position! And O God, how I wished I had died when the bullets hit my chest and my head! At least I would have been saved from this torture which was the worst kind of torture in the world.

When I told Commander Sharhabil about my desire to go back home, he appeared surprised. He tried to make me change my mind. When I insisted, he said, "No one compels a mujahid to put his faith in his religion except his conscience and his obligation to the religious duties of the Law of God, the Almighty, the Exalted. Each has his own circumstances and excuses."

Then, squeezing my hand, he said, "We will talk before you return to your home."

I was bent on returning to Jordan. I had something to do there after what had happened to me.

But I didn't expect Commander Sharhabil to agree so easily.

## Abu Hudhayfah

Darrar surprised us with his decision to return to his family and home.

Commander Sharhabil said to him, "Could it be that you're frightened after being shot by the enemy?"

"Yes," Darrar said. "I am frightened . . . Frightened I will die from an assassination and not as a martyr for the sake of God."

"It's OK, Darrar," I said to him. "When misfortune comes, fear of it creates another misfortune. Be patient and bear it. Stay here in this blessed shelter where the blood of the mujahideen mingles together in the soil. Don't you see that God's watchful eye has healed your wounds and your tongue without any hospital?"

Commander Sharhabil said to him, "What is the value of life if you don't find something in it to fight for?"

"Give me any mission to carry out in my homeland and I am ready to do it," he replied. "Jihad is not confined to only one land, and Paradise opens itself to martyrs wherever they fall."

That statement of his caught my attention. I remembered the conversation with Commander Sharhabil about it later on.

Our attempts to stop him didn't bear fruit. It seemed the attempt to kill him had an effect on his psyche. When Commander Sharhabil was certain he would go back to his home, he sent a gift for his own mother along with him and explained how to get to her shop.

His gift to his mother was one of the spoils we took when we raided one of the regime camps. It was a heavy gold chain with a pendant inscribed with the name of Allah in thick Naskh calligraphy that he found in the pocket of a dead soldier after stripping him of his weapons and ammunition.

As I walked with Commander Sharhabil in the camp, under the light of the full moon, I said to him, "I don't understand why Darrar insists on returning to his family."

"All the light of the universe cannot uncover what's in the darkness of a man's heart," he said. "The darkness of the depths." Then he suddenly corrected himself, saying, "Except for the light of faith, which ensures the dissipation of darkness from all places."

I said, "Did you notice that Darrar said, 'Give me any mission to carry out in my homeland'?"

"Clarify," he said.

"I believe you should look after Darrar before he goes back home. Who knows what the future has in store for us?" I suggested he give him some financial support, to help him get by as he moved on, and to make him feel connected to us.

He asked me, "Can jihad and loyalty be bought with money?"

"No," I said. "But money has been one of the weapons of war throughout the conquests of Islam."

The day Darrar left us, the financial officer came and took him aside in Commander Sharhabil's tent.

## Sari Abu Amineh

What would I tell the Basha?

After we finally got rid of that scoundrel Darrar al-Ghoury, I got word from Yasin, the one who killed Darrar, that Walid wasn't really dead like Darrar had told me. And I learned that the picture of the suicide attack that he sent me was just a fabrication designed to make me think he had done the job I hired him to do.

Walid was still alive. But the Basha thought he was dead.

It was as though one thing constantly led to another, relentlessly. As though heaven wanted to fulfill Uroub's prediction by force, or was helping fate to carry out its mission.

There was nothing to put one at ease, and I no longer had the strength to face the Basha with news like Walid was still alive.

O God, O God. If the Basha only knew.

The Basha called me on the phone and said, "Come quickly."

I went to him. He sat me down beside him and said, "Are you sure Walid was killed?"

"Of course, Basha," I lied. "Walid is dead."

"Why do I feel he isn't dead?" he asked angrily.

"Maybe it has something to do with blood relations, Basha," I said.

He scratched the back of his neck with his fingernails. "I don't understand."

"The blood bond that connects you to Walid," I clarified. "Maybe that's what is giving you that feeling."

His eyes widened and he gave me that look that always frightened me. "I don't think you believe what you are saying," he said.

Then he looked towards the window, in a way that made me feel he was waiting for something to happen.

## Darrar al-Ghoury

When I went to Commander Sharhabil, the financial officer was in his tent. He greeted me politely and then handed me a bundle of money and said, "That which God bestows upon us is *halal* for all mujahideen. Take this assistance. Maybe it will help you at home, for you are one of the ones who are true to their religion and their beliefs. Commander Sharhabil has praised you and sets high hopes on you wherever you may go."

I tried to give the money back, but a cloud of anger appeared on Commander Sharhabil's face.

I signed the financial officer's document and he locked it up in his leather case. Then he got up and reached out to shake my hand, saying, "May God protect you, Darrar. Good luck."

He left the tent and I remained behind with Commander Sharhabil.

He sat me down beside him and then took out a little notebook from his pocket in which he wrote down the address of my house in Mashari', and my phone number, and gave his blessing for my return home. Then he said, "You know, Darrar, our jihad never ends, and it is not restricted by time or place. Syria is not our final destination, and you are one of us no matter how far you go. Who knows what the days have in store? Go with the blessings of God to your home. We will remain brothers in jihad no matter where we end up."

Then he hugged me close; I could feel the trembling beat of his heart.

I said my goodbyes to Abu Hudhayfah and the other mujahideen in the camp — those men with whom I lived the bitterness of life, and its sweetness, if there was anything sweet about it.

I started looking all around me, at the hills and the distant houses, at the trees and the rocky chain of mountains and the stones, the tents and the ditches, the threadbare clothes, the utensils spread out on the ground. My heart stopped and I felt weak.

O God! How difficult it was to say goodbye to the mujahideen, even in my condition.

It took me a full day and a night to reach Daraa, switching onto four different trucks along the way, and a cart pulled by a black mule. The trucks transporting me and several other people who'd been displaced from their homes stopped twenty-three times, at checkpoints and fortifications set up by mujahideen from various squads. I knew them by the mottos they had painted in black letters on barrels, and by the flags they had stuck into the barrels and fastened to their pick-up trucks.

I crossed the Jordanian border through Al-Ruwayshid, with a masked Syrian smuggler whose name and address I had gotten from one of the Syrian mujahideen before leaving the camp. He let me ride behind him on his motorcycle that didn't have any fenders, after I gave him 10,000 Syrian liras.

I was amazed by the smuggler's driving skills. He followed a path he knew well that was covered with parallel and crisscrossed tracks from tires of similar motorcycles. I saw dozens of men, women, and children along the way, speeding headlong towards the Jordanian borders. Their clothes were tattered, their children were screaming and crying, and the women's faces were filled with such pain and sorrow it broke one's heart. As for the men, the way they looked at us seemed to be envying us the luxury of riding on motorcycles that could speed past them.

I was not expecting to be smuggled across the border with such ease and simplicity. In fact I never saw any crossing point and no one stopped us at all. When I got off the motorcycle in the town of Ruwayshid with my linen sack hanging from my shoulder, a service taxi driver approached me, saying, "Amman . . . Amman."

I followed him to his car and he took me and three other passengers to the north transportation station in Amman, for fifteen dinars, which I'd handed to him before we set out.

# Muntaha al-Rayyeh

A skinny young man who said his name was Omar came to see me at my shop. He had a dark face with a horizontal scar across his forehead and the whites of his eyes were the color of a dried-out lemon. He had a light scraggly beard, only four fingers on his right hand, and was the type that made whoever was looking at him feel he was fidgeting and trying to pull himself together.

He spoke to me without looking me in the eye. The entire time while he was talking he looked down at the floor tiles. He said he had come on behalf of al-Walid and handed me a gold pendant with *Allah* inscribed on it.

"This is a gift from Walid. And he asks if the scent of perfume oil in his room that you used to clean is still there or has it disappeared?"

What that fellow said was the best proof that he had truly come on al-Walid's behalf, because no one knew about the incident with the smell of perfume oil in his room except for him and me.

With a joyous and welcoming spirit I asked him, "How were you able to find the shop?"

"He gave me the name of the shop and of the street and told me how to find it," he answered.

I told myself that this meant that al-Walid and the people he was with were keeping an eye on us from a distance, without our knowledge.

I sat him down on the other side of the counter and asked him to tell me everything about al-Walid: Where was he? What was he doing? Was he eating well? Who was washing his clothes for him? I didn't stop asking questions until he showed me on his cell phone screen a picture of al-Walid that he had taken a few days before returning.

In the photo, al-Walid looked thin, and had his long beard and his hair wrapped in a black headscarf. He looked much older than his age, to the point that I thought he might be suffering from some illness, like anemia maybe. But Omar assured me he was healthy and strong-willed, and he pointed out that ten years among the ranks of the mujahideen would cause any man to lose a lot of weight.

He told me that al-Walid had been promoted and was now a commander on the battlefield. He also spoke about al-Walid's heroic deeds and praised them immensely, with great pride and confidence, as if the only thing I was concerned about was bravery, attacks, and hitting tanks with rockets, when all I wanted to hear about was when he was going to come back to me.

"Mrs Umm al-Walid," he asked, "do you know a man called Sari?"

My heart started pounding.

"A man with a pale complexion came to see me a while back," I said. "His hair was parted. He was around fifty. I don't remember his name. He came to see me in the shop."

He was startled. "That was Sari. What did he want? Why did he come?"

"I remember he asked me about al-Walid," I said.

He asked me if it would be all right to come by again and I told him that would be fine. He paused and then he urged me and made me promise to watch out for Sari. Then he said goodbye, promised to come back to visit as soon as he got the chance, and left.

I realized he didn't give me his phone number or address, so I followed after him calling, "Omar! Omar!" But he didn't respond. When I caught up to him and called his name he finally noticed me. "You didn't give me your phone number," I said.

Looking down at the ground, he said, "No, Mother. It's best for both of us if you don't know my phone number."

"What about your real name? You didn't tell me what it is. If your name was really Omar, you would have heard me calling after you from the moment you left the shop."

"Yes, it's true," he said. "But these are necessary precautions, Mother."

## Samah Shahadeh

Fawaz was no longer capable of uninterrupted sleep.

In the past, he would put his head on the pillow at midnight and wouldn't wake up until seven in the morning.

Seven full hours on the dot.

His hours of sleep decreased ever since our encounter with Uroub. Then they started becoming interrupted. I could see some sluggishness hiding in his eyes behind those eyeglasses.

A few days ago, I woke up and was tiptoeing to his bedroom. When I found him I saw he was wide-awake, not doing anything.

Sometimes he would close his eyes and appear to be sleeping, but I didn't think he was really asleep. Sometimes he would fall into a never-ending coughing fit. But a few days ago he nearly choked. A severe choking fit woke him out of sleep and nearly killed him. I heard him coughing and panting from my room, so I rushed to him. His breathing was belabored, as though the air was caught in his throat. His face became blue-black and his eyes and eyelids turned red. Tears rolled down his face. I brought him some water and was about to call his doctor, but he pointed at me and waved his finger in sharp refusal.

When he settled down, I went and made two cups of anise tea and went to him. I put the tray with the two cups down onto the small table and then sat on one of the chairs there in the room. He got out of bed and sat down beside me in the other chair.

He began to wipe his face and eyes with a wet paper towel. As soon as he was finished, he glanced over toward the window. He seemed distracted.

Lately he had been avoiding looking me in the eye.

"The doctor should have come to see what happened to you," I said.

"It happens to people all the time. Just a choking fit and now it's over."

I proceeded to change the subject. "I find it hard to believe the terrorists have singled you out from among all the dignitaries in the country. What is troubling you? Have you gotten entangled in political wrangling, or have you had a falling out with one of your clients over a large sum of money and you're worried he'll take revenge?"

He took a sip from his cup. Then he sighed and said, "If only the matter had to do with money."

"No matter the reason, it isn't fair to hide it from me. Together we can work out a way to relieve you from whatever is troubling you."

He didn't say anything, so I continued. "What I know is that you don't work in politics and you have no enemies. Unless I am mistaken."

"Is there anyone in this world who has no enemies?" he said.

In past years, Fawaz had a much easier time overcoming obstacles that came his way. Sometimes he even got ahead of events before they happened. He used to tell me – whenever I would ask him how he managed to solve a certain problem – it was his excellent intuition, using that expression he borrowed from my father and always used, "A padlock cannot withstand the power of gold."

Had the power of gold deserted him this time? Or was it that old age had turned gold into a worthless hunk of metal? My thoughts grew slow and sluggish. Maybe his intuition had dulled?

His eyes roamed about the room. Then he said, "What will you do if something happens to me?" He gave a slight show of emotion on saying this.

## Abu Hudhayfah

We caught the person who shot and tried to kill Darrar al-Ghoury and brought him into custody. We nabbed him a few days after Darrar left. How I wished Darrar had stayed with us long enough to see his adversary face to face and take his revenge.

The guards found him near the camp at night. His name was Yasin, and he was a Syrian national, one of the many who had been displaced to Zaatary refugee camp in north Jordan. He confessed during the interrogation that he was the one who tried to kill the mujahid Darrar al-Ghoury, may God ease his path, and under torture he spilled the name of the person who sent him on his despicable mission. He said all he knew was his first name, which was Sari, and had no knowledge of where he worked or for whose benefit he'd been sent.

I thought he told us everything he knew, because Commander Sharhabil undertook the torturing himself, and Yasin kept repeating that all he knew was his name was Sari, and that he got 1,000 dollars from him, near Zaatary refugee camp, in return for killing Darrar. And he would get another 2,000 dollars once he'd done it and come back to the camp. When Commander Sharhabil ordered him to pull the 1,000 dollars out of his pockets and show him, Yasin started crying and said he had given it to his wife in the camp before coming, so she could take care of their three children. Sharhabil blew up in anger and smacked him over the head with the butt of his machine gun.

"I don't think he's hiding anything," I said to Commander Sharhabil. "He's not vying patiently or waging jihad for religion or for any cause; he did it for money."

"Then the only thing to do is kill him," he replied.

Blood poured from Yasin's fingers and head, while his face was pale and trembling. His knees shuddered and he looked pleadingly at the commander who was cleaning out the wax from his ears using a swab meant for cleaning weapons, and scratching the bottom of his chin with the fingernails of his other hand.

But not a chance! Commander Sharhabil chose a very strange death for him: He gave him a spade and ordered him to dig a hole in the very place where he had tried to kill Darrar. When he finished, Sharhabil ordered Yasin to lie down in the hole, and when he did, bullets rained down on him from Sharhabil's machine gun. The smell of gunpowder filled the air. Sharhabil emptied an entire round of ammunition into Yasin's body, which started flopping about inside the hole. Then Sharhabil ordered that Yasin's corpse be covered with dirt before putting his machine gun back on his shoulder and brushing his hands together to clean them off. Then he said, loud enough for everyone who had gathered around the hole to hear, "Let him be a warning to others."

But a sudden feeling of uncertainty came over me, despite my joy at having caught that traitor. It had to do with something Sharhabil had told me before, which was that Darrar knew a Jordanian man named Sari whose name he mentioned a little while back. And he asked me if that bit of information meant anything to me.

I didn't know what to say to him, despite my attempts to piece things together. In the end, that fellow Sari sent Yasin to kill Darrar, according to his confessions. It wasn't unlikely that he was connected to one of the branches of the secret intelligence that were targeting the mujahideen.

I reminded Commander Sharhabil of that information in case it would help us. He fell silent, looked directly into my eyes, and then turned his face right and left, as if sniffing out his surroundings. But he didn't say a word, which was his habit – a habit that so often won him a certain level of obscurity, and elicited much curiosity.

The next day, he doubled up security in and around the camp and changed the nighttime password.

## Sari Abu Amineh

I hadn't lost hope, but I was afraid, because I didn't know where Walid went after Darrar was killed – Darrar, who I'd enlisted for the purpose of frustrating and overpowering fate. And I also hadn't foreseen losing touch with the Syrian Yasin, who killed Darrar. Where had he gone?

I was cut off from Walid's news, and that was what terrified me.

Could they have caught Yasin? Did he confess about me? But what would he confess? Like Darrar, all he knew was my first name. He didn't know where I worked or who I worked for, didn't know where I lived, and didn't have a picture of me, either.

The only real danger was Walid, since if he came to Amman he would be able to figure out who I was through his mother.

Couldn't he have come back to Amman without my knowing?

Everything was possible now that Darrar was dead; news about Yasin and Walid was cut off now that those two were gone.

Once again I had the feeling that death was dancing around me and taunting me. Maybe it would grab hold of me at any moment.

I went to see Umm al-Walid at her shop, which was called Nouveauté Al-Hidaya.

It was a small shop, no more than sixteen square meters in area, and was filled with robes and Islamic women's clothing hanging on pipes and folded in piles on shelves. What was irritating about the shop was that it was located in the heart of Swayleh on the right side of the main road leading to the Jordan Valley region. It was a street teeming with cars and pedestrians with all their noise and commotion, and with a mixture of smells from car exhaust, roasting meat, garbage and chicken reeking in the trash bins.

When I saw Umm al-Walid for the first time, I found myself staring with curiosity at the features of her face. I couldn't erase that image I had in my mind of her – the image of a woman who had surrendered her body to the Basha in a Paris hotel, where he did to her what a husband does to his wife, and possibly more.

And even though she knew I had been privy to her whole story, she hadn't flinched one bit when I confronted her with the fact of her illegitimate son.

More than that, her tone was confident, free of shame, as if what she had done were nothing more than voluntarily submitting to some outdated medical test.

She received me this time with a degree of disdain. There was a lot of force and anger in her voice, more than the time before.

"Praise God for Walid's safe return," I said.

I felt – after a few moments passed – that what I said hadn't sounded good.

She replied after a pause, "Listen, Mr Sari. Don't go looking for evil, for evil knows your address." Then after another pause she added, "I told you you'd be better off staying away from me and al-Walid. Tell that to your boss Fawaz, too."

She finished folding the clothes she was holding without looking at me.

"Mrs Umm al-Walid," I said, trying to appease her, "I've come to help you. If you need any help, I am ready, at the Basha's command. If you want to advance your business or you need any amount of money, we are ready. The Basha never forgets his friends."

She placed what was in her hands on one of the shelves, and leaned on her elbow against the countertop. She looked into my face and said, "Truly I am in need of your help."

"At your service, Mrs Umm al-Walid," I said.

"I want Fawaz's address."

With that I tried to keep calm and asked her, "Why do you want the Basha's address?"

"I can get it myself," she said. "I'm only asking you for it to save time."

"Do you want his address so you can go visit him, for example?" I asked.

She looked away from me and went back to folding a shirt on her table. "Who knows?" she said. "Maybe someone else will pay him a visit."

## Muntaha al-Rayyeh

Even though I had made peace with myself concerning that old, fleeting escapade with Fawaz, I couldn't forget the abuse I'd been subjected to when I tried to call him and when the Porcupine confronted me with his suspicious eyes. Fawaz hadn't bothered to ask after me: Had I gotten pregnant from him? Had my family found out and killed me, for example?

It seemed he was the kind of man who thought a woman who succumbed to a man was dishonorable.

I felt that al-Walid's comrade, who had called himself Omar, had come to do something about Sari or Fawaz. His words were extremely forceful.

Life had become complicated once again.

I felt that in life there were unseen lines and strings that led me and influenced my life without my seeing or feeling them.

Maybe my isolation at home after being widowed caused me to think about life and people's conditions, and about the events I had been through but had not attempted to interpret.

What made my head spin as I sat behind my counter at the clothing shop was that that meager sheikh I had seen when I spoke with Sheikh Abu Muhsin, the imam of the mosque, suddenly came through the door of my shop and said, "*As-salaamu alaykum.*"

Then he sat down on the chair across from me behind the counter without asking permission.

His beard was white and his face appeared long and tiny below his headdress.

"Don't you remember me?" he asked, staring at me with his pitch-black eyes encircled by their red eyelids.

"'God creates forty people with the same looks,' sheikh," I said.

He lowered his head and started fiddling with his prayer beads. "May God have mercy on Abu al-Walid," he said.

"Did you know him?" I asked.

"Yes, and I participated in his funeral – may God have mercy on his soul," he answered.

I looked carefully at his face while he was occupied with his beads. Maybe he did it intentionally so I would examine his features.

Suddenly he looked up at me and said, "You used to call me the Porcupine at the Malco Company where you worked under my supervision."

I felt something akin to an electric shock shoot through my body and stop the blood from flowing in my veins. I found myself slapping my head and forehead with the palms of my hands, and then covering my eyes with them.

The Porcupine!

After thirty years, the manager who used to hit on me and all the other female employees had turned religious? With a beard and short *dishdasha* robe and all? After he had known everything under the sun except God the Almighty?

And he knew Nael! And went to his funeral!

All I could think to do was get myself away from that place. Nothing I could have said or done would have been enough to lessen my shock. Going home was the only solution.

I got up and said nervously, "I want to close the shop, please."

"Is this how you welcome your old boss?" he asked, laughing. "The friend of your late husband, in the shop you inherited from him?"

I stormed angrily towards the door. "Please, before I lock the door."

He didn't move. He cast a glance at me that brought me back to the moment when he first set eyes on me after I got back from Paris. That offensive look.

"What happened to your premature son? Did he find out who his father is?"

He said "premature" sarcastically.

I pulled myself together and said, "Listen, Porcupine. I know that God Almighty can bring life back to decaying bones, but I do not think He would bring them back to life so they can deceive people or avenge themselves on them! What do you want from me?"

He stood up. "Nothing," he sighed. "O God, 'Give admonition in case the admonition profits (the hearer).'[xii] But fortunately, I still have the Malco Company record books, the ones we used to work on together. Do you remember them?"

"What have I got to do with that failure of a company?" I said.

He shook his head. "I was looking through the papers and found some receipts having to do with you: the record of your visa to Paris, the price of the plane ticket, your vacation, travel expenses, and your signature on everything, a copy of your passport with the visa and exit and entry stamps. You know those cursed documents. Would you like copies before I send them?"

I shuddered. "Who are you sending them to?" I asked.

"Al-Walid, of course."

"And so what if I traveled to Paris before I was married?" I screamed. "That's if your mail reaches him!"

"I forgot to mention I have a record of the dates: your trip, your return, your marriage, and your conception of al-Walid. The pregnancy was conceived roughly two months before your marriage, while you were in Paris. His birth date attests to that. May God have mercy on your soul, Nael."

I summoned all my strength. "Are you trying to act as a deputy for God, the Lord of the Worlds, and dole out my punishment yourself? What do you want from me?"

He stood up. "Al-Walid! Is he here now, in Jordan? I want his phone number. And has anyone come to see you on his behalf?"

My voice cracked when I answered, "Al-Walid is in Syria and doesn't have a phone. Nor does he want one. And no one has come to see me on his behalf." Then my voice took on a pleading tone while tears of defeat spilled from my eyes. "What can I do to make you leave me alone?"

"I asked you something, but you didn't answer."

Never in my life had I been made to feel so weak and feeble. I reached for the Holy Quran in the drawer, placed my hand on it and swore, crying, "God bears witness that al-Walid is not here. And that I do not have a phone number for him. And that he sent someone to me on his behalf who called himself Omar. He assured me al-Walid was fine and left. I don't know his address or his phone number. Is that enough, or do you want more?"

He looked me in the face with those eyes of his, which at that moment looked like two dark holes. Then he handed me a slip of paper with Fawaz's wife's phone number on it.

"This is the phone number of Mrs Samah, the wife of Fawaz Basha. You must call her and tell her what transpired between you and her husband thirty years ago. Tell her about your son al-Walid, who is her husband's son. Don't take long. I am waiting."

I tried to find out what his intentions were. "I will call her if that is all I'm being asked to do, as long as you stay away from me and al-Walid in return."

He turned to face me and ordered, "Just call her and never mind trying to bargain."

"But . . ."

"Without any 'but,'" he interrupted. "Do what I tell you to do."

The Porcupine had defeated me. The documents and the dates were all in his possession, according to him. He would send them to al-Walid. He could do it.

Even still, I had decided I would do what he wanted. Maybe he would take pity on my situation, and maybe I would reduce the damages he might inflict on me.

"I will call her. The rest is up to you and your conscience," I said.

He left, laughing, as if he was playing a game. But his laugh was sluggish this time around, and his voice was creaky.

After he left, it occurred to me that all I had to do was make a simple phone call to Mrs Samah. Then I tried to sweeten things for myself and thought: calling her was essentially my way of taking revenge on Fawaz.

My throat was dry. I drank a glass of water.

What was the Porcupine's connection to Fawaz's wife? Why did he want me to call her? What did he stand to gain? And why would he want to tell al-Walid about his mother? Why had he appeared now?

I closed up the shop and went home. I felt unable to focus my eyes on the sidewalk anymore. My back hurt and when I reached the house I went inside, locked the door behind me, and cried. I took two of the tranquilizers the doctor had prescribed for me the year before, fell asleep, and slept through to the next morning.

When I woke up the air in my room smelled stale. I opened the window and didn't know what I should do.

I thought about the Porcupine again. He wanted to harm me and harm al-Walid. But why after all these years? Was it because I slapped him when he made a pass at me in his office?

That seemed like a silly reason, too trivial to warrant what he wanted to do. The Porcupine wanted to send all the documents to al-Walid. He wanted to use him to kill me and use me to kill him. But why?

Did he hope to punish me for what I did in Paris, now that he had become devout?

But what would he gain?

I went to the shop. I opened the door and sat down inside. I propped my chin on my palm. Was time really so persistent?

What happened to me was God's judgment and divine decree. But why did this fate keep chasing after me wherever I went? Hadn't it finished with me yet?

As I was thinking, Sari entered the shop. He offered to help me, in accordance with Fawaz's instructions. I answered him sharply and sternly. But when I asked him if he knew the Porcupine he denied it in a manner that made me believe him.

When Sari left, I got the feeling he was afraid or angry. Most likely afraid.

He stood at the doorway after going outside the shop. I saw him get into a black Jeep with wide tires. When he started it, I felt the rumble of the motor was different from the small cars and buses that usually passed down the street. Then I caught a glimpse of Omar, al-Walid's comrade, just as Sari's car started to take off. He was on a motorcycle trailing behind Sari's car.

A new piece of the puzzle, I said to myself. O God, help and preserve us!

# Samah Shahadeh

A woman called me who said her name was Muntaha, Umm al-Walid.

She had a deep, gentle voice. At first I thought she had dialed the wrong number, so I said, "You have the wrong number, Mrs Umm al-Walid."

"Is this Mrs Samah, the wife of Fawaz al-Shardah?"

Fawaz al-Shardah? It had been many long years since anyone had dared refer to Fawaz that way!

"Fawaz Basha," I corrected.

"Doesn't matter, just as long as you are his wife. Did he ever tell you he has a son named al-Walid?"

At first I thought she was some woman trying to get money out of us and that some new conspiracy was being hatched against Fawaz.

"Mrs Umm al-Walid," I said to her. "I don't have time for nonsense."

I was about to hang up but then I heard her say, "I will tell you something to make you believe what I'm saying."

It took a lot of effort to gain control of my nerves, but my curiosity gave me pause. Then I asked her, "How can I be sure of what you claim?"

She answered confidently, "Fawaz has only one testicle, you and I know that, but he is able to have children. At any rate, his son's name is Walid. He's my son, too."

I had no idea what to say to this woman who had shocked and stunned me with what she said. Fawaz did have only one testicle, not two, it was true. And the woman spoke with such certainty.

I couldn't bear to hear any more, so I hung up the phone, but didn't forget to save the number that woman called me from.

If she was lying to me, then that was a problem, and if what she said was true, then it was a bigger problem!

Either way, that woman, who said her name was Muntaha, meaning "utmost," was indeed a woman of utmost evil.

I thought about hurting her somehow, since I had her cell phone number, but then I regretted even thinking such a thing. She was not worthy of my hurting her. If I did that, I'd end up hurting myself.

I decided to wait until nighttime to talk to Fawaz about it.

He was in his office, engrossed in a phone call. I got the feeling he changed the subject when I entered the room. Then he hung up.

I said very calmly, "I received a strange phone call today. A woman who said her name was Muntaha, Umm al-Walid."

I watched his face and eyes in case I caught him in a moment of hesitation or confusion. But he didn't show concern or act as though it meant anything to him.

"What did she want, this woman called . . . What was her name?" he said.

"Muntaha, Umm al-Walid," I said.

He shrugged it off, saying, "OK, that's nice. How old is she? What's her story?"

"Her son is around thirty years old," I said.

"Oh, so she's elderly. Maybe she is one of those social cases they're trying to get us to give money to."

My voice took on a sharp tone. "Fawaz, this woman knows you only have one testicle, not two!"

He was quiet for a moment and then he said without any confusion, "Has the situation with beggars trying to cheat people out of their money reached the point where they've starting delving into people's medical records?" Then he continued. "Didn't she tell you what she wanted?"

"I hung up on her before I could find out. But I saved her phone number. Do you want her phone number?"

He looked at me in disbelief. "What's wrong with you, Samah? What would I do with the phone number of some woman I don't know? I suggest you give her some money so she'll leave you alone."

"She told me that her son is also your son. Doesn't that mean something to you?"

"Yes. It means beggars have developed their methods to an astonishing level."

The next day I felt a longing to see my father. A sudden longing.

## Sari Abu Amineh

Umm al-Walid talked to me in a manner I didn't like at all when I went to see her two days ago. She was angry and agitated. I was almost certain her son had been smuggled across the borders and was now in Amman.

She asked me about someone called "the Porcupine." That was his name. When I denied knowing him she seemed surprised. And she didn't tell me who this Porcupine was when I asked her.

Could luck really be so set against me? Could heaven just fold its arms and step in to insure the fate that was in store for the Basha during his year of sorrow?

I didn't believe in fate in the past, but I was afraid of it.

Now I believe in fate and fear it at the same time. And I believe that fate is cruel and mocking and hatches out plans . . . Fate is greater than me and greater than everyone. And I am nothing but a tiny creature caught up in its mighty, legendary expanse.

I told the Basha everything, for the situation had gotten way beyond keeping such dangerous information to myself. I made it clear I was ready to take full responsibility for my own failure, even if it meant being fired from my job. And that was a mistake that only made things worse. He interpreted the situation not as a matter of my taking responsibility for failure, but rather of shirking responsibility when the circumstances got difficult.

Actually, I thought a lot about the mess I had gotten myself into, not against the Basha or to denounce him in any way, but because my life was in danger.

The Basha seemed perplexed to me as he walked beside me in his garden. As usual he had his hands clasped behind his back. The guard was patrolling the western wall.

This time he was looking around at things and up at the sky with eyes that seemed laden with questions. Even when he looked at me I felt there was a kind of cryptic doubtfulness in his eyes.

He spoke to me in a tone that gave the impression his words were drifting on a floating surface; it was more philosophical than curious. "If Uroub hadn't said those things to me the night of my sixtieth birthday, would it have been possible for everything that happened to happen? Would it have been possible for us to travel to Mumbai, and to send someone to kill Walid – that fellow called Darrar? And would I have surrounded my house with all those security guards? And avoided my wife's looks and questions? Would it have been possible for us to be standing here, on this very spot, having this conversation?"

"No, definitely not," I said.

He came to a stop. "That means that by making her predictions Uroub stirred up the fates."

I thought about this conclusion, which seemed plausible to me. "Logically, it's true."

He lifted his head and looked up at the blue skies. "How long has it been since you looked up at the heavens?"

"I don't remember," I said. "But even if I have looked, I am like everyone else – I look without meaning to and without thinking, and then I forget I looked."

Then I added, philosophizing a bit myself, "But when I hear the word 'heavens' I know what it means without looking up."

He went back to asking, "Have you ever imagined what the heavens look like when they're 'brimming with activity'?"

I put my hand over my mouth and squinted my eyes, thinking.

He didn't wait for my answer. "I think the best way to see it, when it is brimming with activity, is to look down at the earth below us and all around us."

That was something Harsha al-Hakim had not said.

## Darrar al-Ghoury

If my suspicions were correct, then Sari still thought I was dead.

I didn't kill Sharhabil as I had been sent to do. Not because I didn't have a good opportunity. On the contrary, numerous opportunities to kill him had presented themselves to me. But I didn't do it. Something deep inside me diverted me from fulfilling that dreadful mission.

Between this world and the hereafter there is a mandatory strait we all must pass through, and Sari and his money would not be of any benefit to me when my time came. And Sharhabil said, "O Sariyah! The mountain, the mountain!"[xiii]

It was divine inspiration from God Almighty.

And who was I to be the wolf that catches the lamb?[xiv] How would I stand before the face of my Lord?

And more than all of this, I never expected Sari to be behind the contemptible attempt to murder me. He had to pay the price of his wickedness and the corruption of his soul.

When I visited that great lady Umm al-Walid, I took the name Omar as a precaution.

My wound was nearly healed, and I had removed the bandages.

Umm al-Walid told me Sari had come to see her. I thought to myself that he was going to bring about his death all by himself; he was in fact my whole reason for returning.

Umm al-Walid is an upright woman. She clearly loves her son and is anxiously awaiting his return. But he never once expressed any desire to go back home.

I rented a motorcycle and parked it a few meters away from Umm al-Walid's shop on the main street in Swayleh. I began watching the area without drawing attention to myself. I'd buy little things from this or that shop, and I'd go back and put my purchases into the storage compartment of the motorcycle. Other times I would shop around and look at the clothes in the nearby shops, giving myself an opportunity to observe who was going in or out of Umm al-Walid's shop.

I watched for two days, and on the third day – it was a Saturday – I saw the target Sari park his black Jeep right out in front of the shop, get out of the car, and enter the shop. It was late in the afternoon, and I thought to myself that relief was on the way, God willing.

I waited twenty-two minutes for him, and when he came out of the shop and took off in his Jeep, I followed him on my motorcycle, leaving enough space between him and myself to dispel any suspicions.

He continued along the wide street towards Kamaliyya and then headed north along a narrow road. His car climbed up a hill leading to a big house that looked quite luxurious from a distance. Then the car disappeared into a garage with a heavy iron gate. So I turned around on my motorcycle and parked it among the cypress trees where it wouldn't raise suspicion.

I watched the road and waited. Three hours passed before I saw the Jeep coming down from the direction of the house towards the main road, with the target driving.

The following two days I kept surveillance and noted at what times he came and left. The times weren't regular, but still gave me the opportunity to carry out what I was determined to do.

In Afghanistan I had been trained in how to set explosives with timers and ignite them from a distance using wireless pulses, fuses and electric charges.

I prepared the receiver and connected it to an explosive weighing five kilograms. I ran the orange and red light test to make sure it was working. Then I went to the side road leading to the big house, the one the target Sari had driven up in his car previously.

I found a pothole in the asphalt, large enough for the bomb. I buried it and covered it with some little tender pine tree branches – they looked like they had fallen from their mother tree onto the road – and went and hid with my motorcycle a couple hundred meters from the bomb. This way I could use binoculars to see the target approaching and then send the explosive impulses the moment he got to the bomb.

I waited from late afternoon until the evening *maghrib* prayer. I saw the streetlights on the side road come on and was relieved to know I would be able to discern Sari's car from other cars that might come down the road.

An hour passed. Two hours. No cars came down the road except for a few that were not the target I was looking for.

I said to myself that patience was the key to relief.

The place was completely empty of houses and people, and was quiet except for the whooshing of the wind as it brushed the tops of the cypress and pine trees. I looked up through the trees at the dark sky.

I asked for God's forgiveness and recited three of the short *suras*. And I waited.

## Samah Shahadeh

I went to my father's house. I found him in the living room with a man sitting beside him wearing a white *kufiyyeh* with black *igal* cord wrapped around it. He had a tiny face and wore a short *dishdasha* robe and had a set of brown prayer beads in his hand. He stood up to greet me, placing the palm of his hand over his chest indicating his abstention from shaking hands with women.

He was very short and skinny. His general appearance did not put one at ease. Despite that, there he was sitting with my father in his home.

He looked towards my father with conniving eyes and told him he should be going, so my father walked him to the door.

Something about the way the man looked at my father gave me the impression they were in collusion.

I said to him in protest, "I know our lives these days are full of surprises, but from where do you know that wicked-looking man? Since when do you bring this type of person into your home?"

"Bravo, Samah," he said in a congratulatory tone.

"I don't understand," I said. "What's the occasion for this 'bravo'?"

"The occasion is that what you said is true. The Porcupine is wicked. And life these days is full of surprises. And I suspect you will witness many more of them."

Then he explained, "The name of that man who was here is 'the Porcupine.'"

## Darrar al-Ghoury

It got to be nearly nine o'clock at night and I continued to wait beneath those trees that exuded the smell of cypress and pine.

I saw the lights of a car coming down the paved road I had booby-trapped. I got ready. The car came closer, and I could hear the sounds of young men and women singing. When the car and everyone in it came within view of my binoculars, I could see that it was an open convertible and that there were two young men and two unveiled women riding inside – may God curse all four of them! It was the epitome of sacrilege.

The car went off into the distance, their voices faded, and silence was restored.

I thought about what I would do once I'd accomplished my task. I said to myself that I would become an anonymous fieldworker in one of the farms in the Valley, until things changed. Maybe I would run into Sharhabil or Abu Hudhayfah or one of the other mujahideen right here in our hometown. Maybe God would shelter me with His grace and guide my life according to His will. The important thing was that Sari would not be able to get to me, because he would die in the very near future, God willing.

The sound of a car motor came within my earshot. I had heard that muffled rumble before from Sari's car. It was the same sound. I prepared the detonator. All I had to do to ignite the explosives was press the send button.

The Jeep appeared, with the target Sari inside. I saw him and recognized him through my binoculars when the light from the street reflected onto his face. But he was not alone in the car. There was another man sitting beside him. He could be innocent. But the time to act had come, and the target Sari was only seconds away from the bomb, and I simply had to carry out the plan.

As the target came within just a few meters of the spot, I said *"Allahu akbar"* and *"Bismallah"* and pressed the detonator switch. The bomb exploded at exactly the moment the target was passing over it.

The sound of the explosion was loud and resounded through the quiet of the night. A fire was sparked and the blaze shot up like lightning carrying the car with it up into the sky before it dropped back down, flipped over, and rolled to a stop.

I praised God and took off immediately on the motorcycle and headed down an unpaved road that led to the Valley, which I had scouted out previously. I was overcome with the excitement of my victorious accomplishment, and of getting rid of that deceitful Sari who deserved much worse than what I'd done to him.

As for the passenger who was riding with him, his fate had led him to his end at that moment. Maybe he was of the likes of Sari, and maybe God had sent him with him, to find his death.

## Samah Shahadeh

There was a sudden flash of light near the cypress trees that broke the darkness of the night. A fire broke out that was accompanied by a loud explosion that shook our house so hard a vase fell off the shelf and smashed onto the floor tiles. And the plants hanging from the ceiling of the balcony, where I was standing and talking on my cell phone with a friend of mine, were set into motion and started swinging back and forth.

I saw the driver and the guards run frantically towards the Mercedes, get inside, and take off. Only one guard stayed behind who readied his weapon and stood on alert.

I quickly wrapped my robe around me, headed to my car, and followed after them.

Sari's car was flipped upside down. The car body was mangled and the doors had been ripped off and two of the tires had landed several meters away.

I saw the guards – in the car headlights they were shining onto the remnants of the Jeep – pulling Fawaz and Sari out from inside the car, drowning in blood. I started screaming and yelling, slapping my face and pulling my hair, and then I passed out and fell to the ground.

I came to in the hospital. My father was standing over my head. He told me that Fawaz had survived the assassination attempt but would need to undergo surgery.

He told me that Sari had also survived and that they had sewn his abdomen back up after putting his intestines back inside, and that one of his legs had been severed or they were going to have to amputate it.

My father was completely unemotional as he spoke. He was gray.

I felt like I'd aged twenty years. My body no longer had the strength it used to have.

For me to witness an explosion and wreckage of that magnitude was not simply an event I experienced. Rather it was a scene that forced me to take a new look at life itself, and at love and hate, and the gifts of sleeping and waking and laughing, and everything I had taken for granted. It meant that there was more to life than just having fun, and going to evening parties, and reading, and swimming, and traveling, and being happy.

In life there was a quiet hell I had never thought about before.

My father said something very strange. He asked me, "Have you looked in the mirror?"

"No," I answered.

So I got out of bed and he walked beside me. I went into the bathroom and looked at my face in the mirror. I had left the house with messy hair and no make-up, hoping no one I knew would see me. I was in a horrible state.

I went back to my bed and he said something even stranger. "You should have put on some decent clothes, and fixed your hair, and looked after your appearance before leaving the house."

I peered into his face, trying to tell if he was serious. "It seems you've forgotten I rushed out of the house in my robe immediately following the explosion."

Without hesitation, he said, "No, I didn't forget. But you could have taken a little more time."

"And Fawaz?!" I said.

He winked with his right eye. Then he got up to leave, saying, "I'll ask them to get your hospital release papers ready. You'll be going back home today."

"And Fawaz?" I asked urgently.

He left the room without answering.

Sari's wife came to see me. She seemed surprised by my appearance.

"There are police everywhere," she said. "Outside the hospital and up and down the corridors. They're questioning Sari despite his having lost his leg. They want to know who's behind the crime. How could he know when he was the one driving the car? Why didn't they go after the criminals?"

I felt that Rasha was really angry about what happened, and that she wanted to place the blame for what had happened to Sari on us.

## Sari Abu Amineh

The sound of the explosion was still ringing in my ears. And the smell of gunpowder still lingered in my nostrils despite all the medications, hygienic cleansing, and sterilization of my wounds and my whole body.

My ears were still ringing, and I still felt that fear of the end that overcame me the moment of the explosion.

I remembered now, after seeing death with my own eyes, that I killed a man named Shaher al-Zarman, or Darrar al-Ghoury as they called him before his death. True I didn't kill him with my own hands, but I was the one who sent Yasin to kill him!

If I hadn't done that, then Darrar would still be alive and well today.

How did I turn into a killer from afar?

Was this a part of fate's plan that never wanted to end? Or was it part of its mockery that people talked about all the time?

Even Yasin, the Syrian fellow whose family lived in Zaatary refugee camp hadn't come back from the mission I sent him to do. And he didn't collect the rest of the money I promised him.

How heavy-handed fate is!

A simple change in daily routine nearly cost me my life and lost me my leg.

If the Basha hadn't taken a ride with me in my car to go to his appointment at the Four Seasons Hotel at the Fifth Circle in Amman, then I wouldn't have fallen into Walid's trap, and my stomach and chest and arms wouldn't have been torn apart, and the hot, twisted metal wouldn't have severed my right leg, which I have no idea what they did with.

I bled a lot of hot blood. A chunk of my intestines spilled out and I held onto it with my hands until the guards came and took us to Isra' Hospital, the nearest one available.

The Basha bled a lot too. His whole body and clothes were soaked in blood. He fell unconscious and didn't come to for several hours, as I found out.

The doctors extracted more than seven chunks of metal from my body, and little pieces of shrapnel that looked like bullets from a BB gun, and placed them all in a vial. I saw them myself.

I can still feel some force lifting me up into the air and then throwing me down onto the hard ground, then flipping me over and tossing me around. My head hits the car metal and the steering wheel presses down on my hand, and my leg is severed, and my guts spill out, and the hot blood flows over my face and my chest and between my thighs.

I still remember the look of terror in the Basha's eyes the moment of the explosion, the look of someone going to the land of no return.

And so the prediction of Uroub the fortune-teller had come true. Here was fate roaming around in its own backyard. Here were heaven's activities teeming in our country, exactly as Harsha al-Hakim had said.

Walid was in Amman; that was certain. He was the one who wanted to kill the Basha. I was merely an unfortunate companion, one of the ordinary people fate pays little attention to. My name might not even have made its list, for I was merely a tiny cog among millions and billions of wheels by which the mighty machine called fate rolled along its path. Removing me made no difference at all.

Surely Walid found out we didn't die. The details were all over the news and made the front page of the newspapers, so I was told.

So then fate would have to turn itself around, after having gone on its way believing it had completed its task. It would come back for the Basha to finish what it started, and it would use Walid once again to finish off his father. And heaven, which had disregarded the Basha all the years of his life, would ensure fate's success. It would step in, in order to help fate dole out what had been planned for him.

That was what Uroub the fortune-teller said, and that was what was happening.

I was simply an individual who happened to be in the place and time that fate chose to carry out its plan for the Basha. Maybe for this reason I didn't die.

Who knows? Maybe it would seek me out when it came back for the Basha!

If Uroub hadn't turned up in our lives, would things have transpired in this dreadful way? Would it have been possible for my body to be shattered and for me to lose my leg?

## Muntaha al-Rayyeh

I learned that Fawaz al-Shardah had been the target of an assassination attempt. I saw a picture of him on TV that was shown during the news broadcast. I saw the black Jeep flipped upside down, and all the destruction around where it happened. I think it was the car Sari drove to come see me at the shop. And the anchorwoman mentioned that Fawaz's public relations director had been with him when the explosion occurred. I knew it was Sari.

However, despite everything I'd seen, they both escaped death. That was what the anchorwoman said when she described the incident as "a failed assassination attempt."

The next morning, at six a.m., I heard someone knocking at my door. I was getting ready to go to work at the shop. I opened the door and found an officer and three armed policemen, their weapons aimed at me and at the door, their eyes looking left and right.

"Is your son Walid still asleep?" the officer asked.

Before I could answer him, he signaled for the three policemen to enter the house. They searched it thoroughly: the bed, the closet, the kitchen cabinets, the washer, the refrigerator, the oven, the boxes, everything. They even slashed the pillows open and pulled out the stuffing. When they didn't find anything, the officer looked at me menacingly and said, "Don't you want to confess and tell us where he's hiding?"

"Don't trouble yourself," I answered. "And don't waste your time. I haven't seen al-Walid for more than ten years."

"Give me the keys to the shop where you sell clothes," he said.

"I'll go with you," I said, handing him the keys. "I open the doors in an hour."

"God is the one who opens all doors," he said sarcastically. "You'll go with us to the police station. Who knows? You might make it back in time to open the doors to your shop once he turns himself in. That is if we don't find him at the shop."

They took me away in the police car after confiscating my cell phone. A number of men and women looked out the windows of their neighboring houses with curiosity. God knows what they were thinking and saying.

We reached the shop and they got out of the car in a rush. The three policemen took position at each side of the door with their weapons, and when the officer opened the door, they plunged inside as if there were some kind of monster or ghoul in there.

When they didn't find anything, they locked up the shop, gave me the key, and took me with them.

They shoved me through the door of the police station with contempt. They showed no concern for my age or that I was a woman. One of them pushed me into the police chief's office.

But the chief stood up the moment he saw me. He reprimanded the officer and apologized, politely greeting me with respect. He went on to explain it was all just a misunderstanding and he would return me to my home, in an honorable and respectful manner, in a private car, as soon as I finished my tea.

The officer who had supervised the search of my house and my shop entered the office a few minutes later, greeted his chief, and then came over to me and handed me my cell phone.

"Here you are, madame," he said politely. "We treated you unfairly. There was a misunderstanding. It was all a mistake. Very sorry."

I no longer considered anything out of line. After everything that had happened to me, I'd begun to feel that life was just one long series of explosions and astonishing events and I was used to it.

"But you asked about my son!"

"By mistake. Believe me."

When I got back home I started thinking, how could they ask me about al-Walid, search my house and my shop, threaten me with going to jail, then apologize to me and say, "It was all a mistake," and let me go?

I called Mrs Samah, Fawaz's wife, and congratulated her for Fawaz's well-being, not because I was happy about it, but because I wanted to know if he was going to live or die and whether she or one of her acquaintances had stepped in on my behalf to get me out of the police station.

But it was clear she hadn't done anything. She had no idea what had happened to me.

"If I were in your place," she said, "I'd tell my son to flee the country."

"Al-Walid did not come to Amman, Mrs Samah," I said.

Words came out of her mouth like a firecracker. "Then who tried to kill the Basha and Sari, if it wasn't your son?"

"Why would a son want to kill his father?" I asked.

She was silent, and then she hung up.

Most likely, that fellow who came to see me who said his name was Omar was the one who did it.

My phone rang. It was the Porcupine.

He congratulated me for getting released from the police station, and then he praised me for calling Mrs Samah as he had told me to do.

I wasn't surprised; the Porcupine was just one more in the series of life's strange departures around me, which I had gotten used to and didn't surprise me anymore.

"How did you know?" I asked.

He started laughing that childish way of his, but in a voice that sounded like the rattling of a sieve being shaken back and forth. "Didn't you realize I was the one who stepped in to get you released?"

"And why did you step in?" I asked.

"You'd ask this rather than thanking me for doing what I did on your behalf?"

I felt that I had the ability to get back at him for having defeated me. It was a feeling that overcame me at that moment.

"You didn't do it for my sake. You did it for Fawaz, your big boss and everyone else's. You're worried about his position and his reputation if the scandal of me and of al-Walid gets out. Didn't this Fawaz of yours die?"

His laughter disappeared. "Fawaz? I haven't seen Fawaz, and I haven't heard his voice since I left the company. I never liked him, actually, even when I worked for him. He deserves what happened to him and more."

"So why did you get me released, then?" I asked.

"Because I'm not done yet. I might need you. But I have to be honest with you. What you said was correct. Al-Walid didn't come here."

Then he went back to that loathsome laughing of his.

Every day I discovered that life – despite the easiness it showed to me – was extremely complicated in its depths.

When my husband died – may God have mercy on his soul – I was at odds with him. I told him he had caused us to lose al-Walid, and I accused him of pushing him to go to Afghanistan.

He confirmed my accusation, saying, "Would I regret doing something for the sake of God? I told you that if I were his age I would have gone to do jihad before him."

At least he didn't lie about it, or disown what he said.

But there was something that kept nagging at me whenever I remembered that Nael had stood in support of al-Walid going to Afghanistan, and that he was the one who planted those ideas in his head that led him onto that path.

That something that kept nagging at me had something to do with blood. Al-Walid was not Nael's son, was not his flesh and not his blood, as they say. Then a not-so-innocent question came to my mind: Wasn't it possible that was why he never really had a strong feeling of responsibility towards him?

True he believed al-Walid was his son. That topic never came up between us, and I felt that was one of the basic assumptions of his life. But when I saw the Porcupine, after all that time, everything got disrupted. The basic assumptions weren't what they had been.

Wasn't it possible that the lack of a blood tie between Nael and al-Walid played a role in encouraging him to ruin himself with the mujahideen?

That question found some resonance within me, and created a new possibility that terrified me. I felt like my heart dropped from its location in my chest, and went on beating somewhere else. Was it possible Nael had known al-Walid was not his son? So he kept it inside, and then wanted to punish me by sending him to die in Afghanistan and cause me to be distraught by it?

That hadn't occurred to me before.

Could Nael have been so deeply secretive, and spiteful to such an extent?

I recalled numerous situations I thought would help me arrive at the truth. I remembered that he said to me – when al-Walid was just a few months old – that he didn't look like him.

Then Nael had his doubts from the very beginning!

Why hadn't all that occurred to me before? Where was my mind?

And when al-Walid turned six, he told me he didn't look like him at all.

And then the Porcupine told me he knew Nael. They used to pray together, and talk after prayers. And the Porcupine had known my whole story ever since those sinful days.

I changed my clothes and thanked God that al-Walid had not come back.

Then I remembered what my mother had said, "You don't love al-Walid."

Could there be something to what my mother said?

O God! This puzzle was way beyond what my mind could grasp.

My phone rang. It was al-Walid on the line.

Without thinking, I said, "My good boy, I was just thinking about you a minute ago."

Then I filled his ears with lots of expressions about longing and waiting and wishing.

"I miss you, Mother," he said. "May God guide your path."

His voice sounded hurt and carried a kind of sternness, though I didn't understand why.

"When will you come home, al-Walid?"

He was quiet for a little while. Maybe he hadn't heard anyone call him by that name for many years.

"Here they call me Sharhabil," he said.

"It doesn't matter," I said. "I just want to know when you're coming."

A few seconds later he said, "The weather is hot these days."

"It's autumn, and you're in Syria, not the north pole. What's with you, al-Walid?"

I said that and then his voice trailed off again. I felt like he was speaking in brief phrases, without clarifications. Again I asked him, "You didn't answer me. When are you coming?"

He cleared his throat and begged God's forgiveness. Then he said, "I don't know. Our jihad is ongoing. Only God knows when or where we will be tomorrow or the next day."

"Haven't you gotten tired and fed-up with that by now?" I asked.

The sound of his voice grew even sterner. "Say God is one, Mother. May God set you on the path of righteousness. Does a believer ever grow tired of jihad for the sake of God?"

It occurred to me that he had intentionally chosen to call me on that particular day, possibly to tell whoever was tapping my phone that he wasn't coming to Amman, and that he was calling from Syria, not Jordan. So he wanted to protect me, even if he was far away from me.

I said to him, trying to let him know I understood the reason for his call, "I know why you made a point to call today in particular."

His voice sounded more at ease. "You've relieved me from the burden of asking."

Avoiding getting into details, I said, "Your health is all that matters. Take care of your body. Eat well and sleep well."

He cleared his throat. "You didn't answer me, Mother."

"Answer you about what?"

"About the hidden thing, the secret."

I felt he said it flippantly. "The secret? What secret?!"

He continued with a kind of determination, "The secret my father told me to ask about after he died!"

"What secret, al-Walid?!" I asked.

"The day he saw me off around ten years ago, he told me to tell you that he knew what you were hiding from him, but he didn't tell me what it was. He made me swear not to ask you about it until after he died, if God Almighty chose him ahead of me. Are you hiding something, Mother?"

Now I remembered that when al-Walid first called me after Nael's death he tried to ask me about something, but he hesitated and didn't insist. This time he asked, and he wanted an answer.

Before hanging up, I said, "It seems jihad has changed you. Do you really believe your mother was hiding something from your father before his death, and from you, al-Walid?"

I had to admit that I did not know the Nael I had lived with all those years. What had he been thinking? What had been going through his head?

Most importantly, what was it that the Porcupine was planning to do? Why had he appeared to me during my tribulation, like some kind of rash judgment?

It seemed I needed another lifetime to understand life.

# Abu Hudhayfah

Nothing happens in this world except by the divine decree of God Almighty, and all the destinies of all the world's creatures were written before God created the heavens and the earth.

The last battle Sharhabil decided to embark on was at one of the food storage warehouses belonging to the government forces.

The mujahideen were preparing their weapons and ammunition, and had them propped up on their shoulders in the vehicles. The door to Sharhabil's tent was lowered, which I found strange, because it was his practice to oversee battle preparations himself.

I stood at the door, cleared my throat, and called, "May I have permission to enter, Commander?"

I didn't hear any response. I noticed a faint cloud of smoke seeping out of one of the seams in the tent, and dissipating as soon as it hit the open air.

I didn't wait. I raised the door panel, poked my head inside, and saw the most astonishing thing.

Commander Sharhabil was sitting cross-legged on the floor, the palms of his hands over his eyes. He had a vest of explosives strapped on, a machine gun by his side, and in front of him was a pile of burnt papers that were still smoldering. His expression was so tense I thought the smoke from the burning papers had mingled with the smoke I imagined emanating from his fuming head.

I went closer to him. I saw on the floor behind him an envelope that read: *To the honorable Mr Walid Nael Dughaybil (Sharhabil).*

I don't know where that envelope came from or how it reached him. I guessed the burnt papers were what had been inside the envelope.

He moved his hands away from his eyes and stared at the blackened papers.

That man I saw in the tent was not the Commander Sharhabil I knew, not at all. His face was dark and his eyes protruded.

I said to him apprehensively, "With your permission, is there some weighty matter I don't know about?"

He let out a heavy sigh. "There are many matters, but they aren't related to jihad this time. They pertain to me personally, at home."

"Can I hope to assist you with these matters? Would the fact of all these years we've spent together allow me to ask about these things?"

He shook his head and with a look filled with so much tension I could hardly recognize his face, he said, "What is torturing me and tearing me apart about this secret is that I cannot tell anyone about it, not even you, Abu Hudhayfah!"

Then he sighed and with a slight show of relief he added, "I thank God that every problem has a solution, and every crisis has a way out. It doesn't matter whether the way out is above ground or below."

What Commander Sharhabil said was substantial, for he was a man of very few words. But this time he seemed to have a need to talk, and to say something.

I looked again at the twisted, burned up papers in front of him, and at the envelope tossed onto the ground behind him. I tried to understand something of it, but what he had said locked all the doors.

He got up, holding his weapon in his hands. He strapped it to his shoulder. Then he took the anti-tank rocket launcher from the tent post and hung its belt behind his neck so it dangled over his chest.

As he started for the door he said, "Let's go, Abu Hudhayfah. Let's pledge ourselves to either victory or martyrdom for the sake of God. I have a feeling that this pledge will be our last!"

We pledged, and I could see that envelope flip over in the wind that blew in from under the bottom of the tent.

We went out and headed towards the mujahideen waiting for us in their vehicles, with the artillery and ammunition. Sharhabil walked beside me and began to pick up his pace. He got ahead of me and I noticed that his shoulders were much broader than I remembered and his back was thicker and wider.

We started moving in our vehicles that were packed with mujahideen, heavy artillery, ammunition, and rocket launchers. Ten vehicles moved in unison towards the target, led by the vehicle carrying Commander Sharhabil who insisted on sitting on the metal bar behind the heavy artillery on top of the black pickup.

We stopped a few kilometers short of the target: the food warehouse. We waited until the *maghrib* prayers were concluded and then we set out again in our vehicles with our headlights turned off.

We moved toward the warehouse which extended for almost half a kilometer. The gunfire did not come in our direction. A few rounds were fired towards the gate from the heavy machine gun mounted on Commander Sharhabil's vehicle, and other machine guns were fired from our side, but we didn't see anyone at the thick iron gate to the warehouse.

Commander Sharhabil's vehicle circled round the warehouse at high speed, and Sharhabil was clinging to the heavy machine gun mounted on the top of the truck. He started firing at the warehouse's windows; that was the method he always followed for testing out a place before purging and storming into it. But then suddenly his vehicle rushed headlong through the gate — a very hazardous undertaking that broke the protocol of how we battled with our enemies. The place should have been purged with rockets and machine gun fire before entering in.

That foolhardy action caused us to be confused, especially when the rockets started coming, and the sounds of the explosions blasted our ears, and bullets from machine guns poured out from numerous positions inside the warehouse. And so four of our vehicles headed towards the gate and stormed through it while a number of mujahideen and I stayed back in the remaining five vehicles in the surroundings outside the warehouse.

Darkness was slowly settling over the place. In a matter of seconds, the area around the warehouse was transformed into an inferno. Bullets and rockets came towards us from every direction – from the rooftop of the warehouse, from holes in the walls, from windows, and doors. And we were surprised by numerous tanks approaching very close to us that came from a slope on the south side of the warehouse. They were approaching rapidly, and crazily, so we battled them all at once without a clear plan.

I looked for Commander Sharhabil when I saw those armored vehicles, for he was the "slayer of armor." But the battle going on inside the warehouse was much harsher than the one outside. It was at its worst.

We sustained much heavier damages than we expected. They destroyed our vehicles and most everyone inside them was martyred. They took a number of mujahideen prisoners after they ran out of ammunition. Only very few of us remained. The darkness aided us to withdraw and hide in the nearby brush until the reinforcement vehicles we requested arrived to take us back to the camp.

I don't know why I kept feeling that Commander Sharhabil was making a move in some concealed place and would surprise all the mujahideen by changing the course of the battle.

I never considered the possibility of him being martyred or taken prisoner.

We got back to the camp broken and wounded. We looked each other over, one by one. But Commander Sharhabil hadn't made it back with us.

## Sari Abu Amineh

It would have been possible for my stay in the hospital to amount to a kind of forced vacation, during which I could take a break from all the running around and thinking and constant panting, despite my miserable condition.

But how could I relax when I felt that fate was roaming about the hallways and rooms, angrily stomping its feet and breathing its heavy breaths, sucking up all other sounds?

Might it be searching for the Basha?

It was as though my brain didn't believe I'd lost my right leg. It still felt as if it were right there. Both of my knees still trembled, and even though the doctors had managed to stop them from knocking together, they couldn't stop the tremors that had begun right after the explosion.

From time to time, I found my hand reaching over to scratch the toes of that foot that was amputated, as if it hadn't been cut off.

A few hours ago I woke up in intense pain. It felt like my heel was on fire. And despite everything the doctor told me and all of his persuasive proof that my heel was no longer there – because the entire leg had been amputated – it still did not stop my sensation of it being there and of the incredible pain that lasted two full hours.

The Basha survived, but his chest and shoulder and arm and all his ribs were hurt. They sent him to Paris to put his body back together, because the lives and deaths of the rich do not belong to them, but rather to fate's master plan.

That was what Harsha al-Hakim had said.

The thing that frightened me most of all when the explosion happened, apart from the feeling of time suddenly coming to a stop, and the terrifying look in the Basha's eyes – which I had never seen before in the eyes of any creature on the face of the earth – was the hot feeling that spread through every part of my body with lightning speed, the feeling that everything was coming to an end and a powerful desire to see myself in a mirror, to know what had happened to my body.

I didn't think of my son or my daughter or my wife! The only thing I thought of was my body and whether it was still in one piece or whether the explosion had blown it to pieces.

Mrs Samah came to visit me and see how I was doing. I found out that she hadn't gone along with the Basha to Paris while he underwent treatment. That was a first.

I divulged to her everything Uroub had told the Basha, and what the Indian sage had said, as part of an attempt to settle some accounts with myself and others, with life itself, which was something I felt I needed to do, because I couldn't be certain if I was going to stay alive after what had happened.

She listened with great interest. In her eyes I saw indescribable anger and terror. Her face changed colors and reacted distinctively. When I finished talking, she got up, and haughtily turned her face away from me. Maybe deep down she despised me.

Rasha came and put four newspapers on the little table beside my bed.

"What's strange about the Basha's secret is that he was able to keep it from his wife for more than thirty years. Even stranger is that you were able to keep it from me, even though you knew everything. And you men say, 'Mighty is the snare of women'?!"ˣᵛ

Then she shook her head and sighed.

"Listen to me. You don't need to be working with the Basha," she said.

What she said was strange, as if she didn't know I was no longer capable of working and that her advice was coming a bit too late, like giving medicine to a dead man.

I looked at her. Glancing at the newspaper headlines, she said, "You haven't read what the papers are saying about what happened. I brought all of them here for you so you can read them."

I flipped through the pages and found that it was all just the same bit of news repeated in more than one paper under the headline *Terrorist Attack Targets the Basha Fawaz al-Shardah*.

I expected there to be lots of repercussions in the news later on, but I didn't read anything else about it in the days that followed. I sensed that they shelved the topic out of concern for the Basha's safety and his reputation.

I remember now that the Grand Basha, Nayef Shahadeh, was the person originally behind Uroub's surprise visit. When I phoned him ten days prior to Fawaz Basha's sixtieth birthday to invite him to the party, he told me he was aware of the date, but that he was going to be out of the country the night of the party. Then he said, "Too bad! I was going to prepare a surprise of the highest caliber for him on his birthday!"

I politely asked, "Might I ask what that is, sir?"

"I heard about an inspired Moroccan fortune-teller named Uroub," he had said. "She is going to be in Amman the day before the big occasion. I thought about bringing her to Fawaz's house to tell his fortune for him. But what's the use? I won't be able to attend that night."

I asked his permission, saying, "May I have the honor of setting up this surprise myself, sir?"

After a brief pause, he answered me. "OK, Sari. You deserve all the best. But don't ruin the surprise and tell Fawaz Basha. Promise?"

If you only knew, Grand Basha, what your surprise brought down on us in ruin and destruction that were greater than all your riches combined!

Al-Walid didn't die. It doesn't matter that Uroub's prediction was not fulfilled and he didn't kill his father. What matters is that I became one of the people being targeted, and it was quite possible that my demise might come at his hands or the hands of any of his comrades.

It was possible that whoever was carrying out the investigation didn't know anything about Walid or Darrar al-Ghoury or the Syrian Yasin.

Most likely they didn't know anything about Uroub.

Perhaps they didn't think about heaven's activities teeming in our region, making it impossible to impede fate, or change its plan, or make it stray from its path.

# Samah Shahadeh

So that's how it was.

Fawaz was a Don Juan who wasn't satisfied with chasing after women and screwing them, but got one of them pregnant with his illegitimate son!

He might have lots of illegitimate sons, God knows!

If Mrs Muntaha hadn't told me, I wouldn't have known that her son is Fawaz's son. I confirmed that when I called her back and she gave me two new pieces of evidence. She told me that she left deep scratch marks on his back when he slept with her in Paris.

I had indeed seen two big scratches on his back when he returned from his trip to Paris.

She also told me that he had a lot of hair on the backs of his shoulders.

That woman awakened me to the truth, but she arrived too late. Much too late.

Fawaz had become someone else. He had suffered massive injuries and required many surgeries to put his body back together, and get it functioning again, as the doctors said.

They took him to Paris to treat him and fix him. I refused to go with him.

I didn't tell my father about Fawaz and his son. I was embarrassed. I felt insulted. So I chose not to tell him anything.

Most likely he knew everything, though. My father had eyes.

Why didn't I pursue what was behind that dreadful laugh of Fawaz's, the one where his teeth and upper gums show? That laugh that manifested itself before my eyes twice? Once when he returned from Paris more than thirty years ago, and again when I asked him what Uroub told him the night of his sixtieth birthday party.

Sari got what he deserved.

When I visited him in the hospital the second time, he told me about Uroub's prediction and what the Indian sage they went to see said to them.

He told me that surprising Fawaz by bringing Uroub to his sixtieth birthday party wasn't his idea, but had been my father's idea, though he hadn't attended the party that night.

He said it with the tone of someone refuting an accusation made against him.

Maybe I was nicer than I should have been, more patient than I should have been, and had given Fawaz my full and boundless trust too easily. Now I realized there was nothing in this life that was boundless. Even our planet Earth had boundaries. Maybe our entire universe did, too.

My father came to visit me. We sat at a table beside the fountain with the *houri* sculptures. The sky was vast and the day was glaringly clear and the wind was fiddling with the white umbrella over our heads. He looked into my eyes and said, "I've known everything for a long time."

"I suspected so," I said feebly.

My tears started to flow.

He looked up to the skies and said, "It is true that he did what he did secretly, without our knowledge, but fate has punished him twice. Once when he lost his son forever, and again when his car blew up. Do you want more?"

"I heard that it was his son who tried to kill him."

"I think," he said, scratching the back of his right hand with the fingernails of his left, "I think his son died in Syria."

I was gripped by a terrifying feeling concerning the kinds of revelations I was exposed to every day. Every hour, actually. I started asking about everything in a loud voice mixed with a tone of anxiety.

"He died? How? Who killed him?"

"He might have been killed in one of their battles," he answered. "Maybe he carried out a suicide attack. I will know the details soon."

I asked in that same voice, "Then who tried to kill Fawaz?"

"They are still investigating," he said.

"And what about Uroub's prediction?" I asked hastily.

"Since when do you think this way, Samah? Watch yourself," he said.

"But her prediction is the reason why all of this happened!" I said.

He looked at me in astonishment. "Fawaz betrayed you thirty years before she arrived."

I said, with a thought having suddenly sparked and gone up in flames in my mind, "True. But if Uroub hadn't shown up in our lives, then everything that has happened from the night of Fawaz's birthday up until this very moment would not have happened. Am I wrong?"

When he didn't comment, the idea burned even brighter, and in that same anxious, raised voice I said, "I feel as though Uroub is not real, as though she is a lie! Or something of that nature!"

He smiled, and his smile was wide but not innocent. An evil shadow glimmered in his eyes, and from the wrinkles on his face that had formed as a result of that smile came a cloud of fright I could practically touch with my hand.

I lost my sense of place and time. I felt like a feather floating in a bottomless abyss. My brain became like a calculating machine, running heavy analyses of everything that happened. It worked without slowing down. My father was tracking my facial gestures like someone waiting for a patient to come out of a coma.

His cell phone rang. He answered it. "Hello, Porcupine. Great, great. I'll see you tomorrow. We'll talk in the morning."

Then he hung up.

I said to him, again in that anxious, raised voice, "As though *you* are fate . . . Or maybe its accomplice?"

He imposed those blue eyes of his upon mine. "Do you know what the Indian sage said to Fawaz?"

While contemplating what was behind those eyes and those wrinkles of his, I said, "Sari told me everything in the hospital."

He looked up and said, "I like what the sage said to Fawaz. But one thing he said about fate didn't convince me, for Fawaz is not one of the main cogs in the great machine of fate."

# Notes

i    From a poem by poet Ahmed Shawqi, written while in exile from Egypt.

ii    From *Surat Al-Ahzab* (The Clans), Verse 23. Translation from Quran Database: http://www.oneummah.net/quran/book/33.html. Full verse: Among the Believers are men who have been true to their covenant with Allah: of them some have completed their vow (to the extreme), and some (still) wait: but they have never changed (their determination) in the least.

iii    *Qiyam al-Layl*, literally 'standing at night'. Voluntary prayers performed after the *Isha* prayer (last of five obligatory prayers) from the middle of the night until dawn and involving recitations from the Quran while standing. See http://www.ahya.org/amm/modules.php?name=Sections&op=viewarticle&artid=83

iv    *Salat Khauf*, literally 'prayer of fear.' Special prayers performed in shifts during times of fear or danger. See http://www.islambasics.com/view.php?bkID=20&chapter=35

v    From *Surat al-Anfaal* (The Spoils of War), Verse 17. Translation from Quran Database: http://www.oneummah.net/quran/book/8.html

vi    From *Surat Al-Ma'ida* (The Table Spread), Verse 99. Translation from Quran Database: http://www.oneummah.net/quran/book/5.html

vii    From *Surat Al-Waaqia* (The Inevitable), Verse 79. Translation from Quran Database: http://www.oneummah.net/quran/book/56.html

viii    From *Surat Al-Baqarah* (The Cow), Verse 286. Translation from Quran Database: http://www.oneummah.net/quran/book/2.html

ix    A breakfast favorite, consisting of marinated chick peas and fava beans seasoned with olive oil and lemon juice.

x    From *Surat Al-Anfaal* (The Spoils of War), Verse 27. Translation from Quran Database: http://www.oneummah.net/quran/book/8.html

xi  The reference is to Al-Gama'a Al-Islamiyya, the Islamic Group, an Egyptian Sunni Islamist movement.

xii  From *Surat Al-A'la* (The Most High) Chapter 76 Verse 9. Translation from Quran Database: http://www.oneummah.net/quran/book/87.html

xiii  The reference is to Omar Ibn Al-Khattab's Miracle. Omar was giving his Friday sermon in Medina and shouted, "O Sariyah Bin Zunaim, the mountain, the mountain!" Sariya Bin Zunaim was in the midst of battle hundreds of miles away but heard Omar's cry and knew to take to the mountain to shield his troops. The Muslims eventually won their battle with the Persians as a result. For more see: https://books.google.com/books?id=joKZBQAAQBAJ&pg=PT33&lpg=PT33&dq=sariyah+bin+zunaim&source=bl&ots=TYEASkAhML&sig=QGCZbPMVql_6_WscujWioGlGjKY&hl=en&sa=X&ved=0CB8Q6AEwAGoVChMIxNn9joeIxwIVSpmACh2HfQqb#v=onepage&q=sariyah%20bin%20zunaim&f=false

xiv  The reference is to the complete utterance when Omar shouted "O Sariyah Bin Zunaim, the mountain, the mountain! He who is the wolf that catches the lamb is an evildoer." See: https://ar.wikipedia.org/wiki/سارية_الجبل

xv  From *Surat Yusuf* (Joseph), Verse 28, translation from Quran Database: http://www.oneummah.net/quran/book/12.html